FLORENCE WITKOP

SOUL WARS: LEXI

by

Florence Witkop

CHAPTER 1

I reached the cottage with a mixed sigh of happiness and relief. After two days driving a tiny, uncomfortable car better suited for city commutes than long distances, I'd reached the cottage with enough daylight left to unload a few things and make dinner before collapsing for an entire night of wonderful, amazing, dreamless sleep. I might sleep until noon.

I got out of my car and meandered across the yard to look for the key my aunt sneakily hid in a hollow in a stump that was all that was left of a tree that had died years before she'd bought the place. A haughty, ceramic gnome had always sat on top of the stump.

Now, as I crossed the yard, I stopped. Stared in dismay. And gulped. Because instead of sitting on the stump the gnome was scattered about the yard in a thousand pieces. The stump itself was a twisted disaster of rotten wood spread across the front yard in the form of splinters and shards.

Winter storms had obviously been disastrous for

both tree stumps and gnomes.

So where was the key? The windows were locked. Probably double locked with deadbolts, thanks to Aunt Gertrude. "No one is getting in my cottage while I'm away. No robbers. No kids looking for a place to party. Everything is double locked and with deadbolts."

I searched the yard where the stump used to be, hoping to find the key. No such luck. Then, with a look at the sun that was closing towards the horizon while remembering there was no motel in town, I decided desperate situations called for desperate solutions. I'd break into my aunt's cottage.

I could smash a window and replace the glass later. Easy enough. But there was a problem. Though it was a single story building the windows were too high to reach without standing on something. But what?

The only possibilities were my suitcases. So I grabbed a suitcase from the trunk of my car and dragged it to the nearest window. It wasn't enough, I needed more height, a familiar problem for five foot something me. So I dragged a second suitcase to the window and piled it on top of the first one.

Still not high enough. The third and last suitcase, though, would do the job, so all I needed was something to break the window with. Since my new business that I'd be starting soon would involve turning junk into treasures, there was a lot of that in the car. Junk. In mere moments I hefted a heavy metal lamp that needed a shade I'd make. A gorgeous shade because I knew how to do gorgeous.

It was perfect so, lamp in hand, I examined the suitcase pile and reluctantly decided the only way to the top was by climbing and hoping the whole pile stayed in place. It probably would.

Unfortunately, it didn't.

At the worst possible moment, the suitcase pile moved. Tilted. Slid. With me on it. I screamed. Flailed about. Dropped the lamp. And fell.

I never hit the ground because a pair of very strong arms appeared suddenly from behind and caught me. As the suitcases tumbled every which way I lay in those arms and was glad to be alive and very, very safe.

I remembered my manners. I twisted enough to recognize that my savior was a man – though there'd been no doubt about that because those arms were a tribute to muscular male perfection – and said, "Thank you."

The man grunted and turned me to face him. "Who are you and why are you trying to break into a cottage?" Ice blue eyes raked my face and then the rest of me as he said, "You're a thief but you won't rob this place. I'm calling the cops."

I struggled against the arms that held me fast. "I'm not a thief."

"You certainly are." The arms didn't let up, not one tiny bit, as those eyes turned into Antarctic ice. Really cold.

But I managed to talk. Barely. "My aunt owns this

cottage but I can't get inside because the key isn't in the stump." I pointed to what was left of the stump. "Because the stump is toast."

Those ice blue eyes narrowed dangerously. "That's not even close to a believable story."

I sagged in those stalwart arms and tried to think how to convince him I was telling the truth. Then I remembered. "My cell phone." I pointed to the car with my phone on the seat. "There are pictures of the cottage on the phone. And more pictures showing where to find the key. And more of me and my aunt. And I can call her. She'll verify my story."

Those eyes lost some of their ice as their owner pondered my words and those unusually strong arms loosened just a bit as I examined the man who'd rescued me but still might send me to jail

He was the most perfect male I'd ever seen. Slightly over six feet with blue eyes that would surely resemble a summer sky when he wasn't angry, a body that screamed athlete and dark hair cut very short. Current or recent military?

I soon was showing him pictures of the cottage and more of my aunt and me with the cottage in the background and a couple of the tree stump intact with the gnome on top and last of all, of a tiny, almost invisible hole beneath the gnome's left foot with a key in it.

"See the key? I'm telling the truth."

He folded his arms across his chest, stretching an

oldish tee shirt taut that matched tattered shorts that fit as snugly as the shirt. But he wore excellent and rather expensive running shoes. So he was out for an evening run and had seen what he thought was a break-in.

"Call your aunt." Arms still folded, eyes still with remnants of ice, though not as much as earlier. "Maybe then I'll believe you."

My aunt was on speed dial and answered, her voice sleepy and disoriented from the time difference until she saw the picture I'd taken of the destroyed stump and explained the situation. Then she took a deep breath. "There isn't another key." Followed by, "You'll have to break in."

The man beside me coughed. Sighed. Raked his hair except with it so short there wasn't much to rake. And turned kind of red because he was embarrassed, which was exactly how he should feel. "Okay. I believe you." And then he smiled and just like that, the entire day glowed as if the sun had suddenly grown a thousand times brighter than when he'd frowned.

Aunt Gertrude had heard him. "Who else is there? Who are you? Can you help?"

The smile grew and there was a hint of apology in it to match the embarrassment. "Maybe." He tipped his head and inspected me and I saw him decide to turn that almost apology into actual help. "Okay, I'll do it. I'll make sure she gets safely inside."

Aunt Gertrude thanked him effusively and went back to sleep and the hunk beside me looked at the metal lamp lying on the ground nearby. "It'll work." He grabbed it and stepped to the window where, without needing suitcases to stand on, he broke the window. Then he continued until all the glass was gone and I could climb safely through.

"Need a lift?" Before I could answer, those arms were around me once more and lifting me and I soon was inside and moments later I had the door open.

"I don't know what I'd have done without you." I hoped he'd answer with something that I could then turn into an invitation for coffee so I could talk to him longer. Get to know him. Salivate a bit over those muscular and very useful arms. And, most of all, feel good about life in general because I was where I wanted to be and now I knew someone local who was also helpful. And nice. And gorgeous in a male sort of way.

Didn't happen. He shrugged and without another word jogged out to the road and continued with his evening run, leaving me to stare after him and wonder who he was and whether he was married or otherwise taken and a thousand other things I didn't know any more than I knew his name.

I sighed and went inside and found some cardboard and covered the broken window and ate a can of cold spaghetti because after all that had happened, I was too tired to cook. Then I considered sleeping arrangements.

There was one bedroom and a sleeping alcove. I wanted the alcove for an office so I dragged a suitcase into the bedroom. Just one suitcase. The rest could wait, no matter that everything was outside on the grass or in the car. I was that tired.

The bedroom was on the east side of the cottage so the sun would wake me in the morning. I smiled at the thought. Then I climbed into bed and dropped off to sleep expecting to sleep deeply all night long.

~

Around two in the morning by the old fashioned luminous clock on the wall, late enough that I'd got enough rest to be in the lighter phases of sleep, I came suddenly awake. I sat up and stared into the dark and asked myself what had awakened me.

A sound? Was that what had awakened me? Yes, I'd heard something. I was sure of it.

What kind of sound? I listened for it again. And heard a whisper.

"Lexi."

My name. Who knew I was there? I'd not told anyone where I'd be, not yet. Still, someone knew my name and that I was there. And that someone was in the cottage with me. Unannounced. Uninvited. Unwanted.

It came again. "Lexi Tremaine."

"Who's there?" I spoke bravely into the night but I didn't feel brave. Instead I felt the first faint tremors of fear because I was alone, the nearest town was miles away and the other cottages scattered along the lakeshore weren't occupied yet. Too early in the season.

Whoever was whispering my name not only knew who I was they'd somehow got past the locks I was sure I'd clicked into place. All those deadbolts that kept the cottage secure against winter while it was empty. But there was the window with cardboard on it. Yes, that must be how someone had gotten inside.

I was terrified. I pulled the blankets to my neck because it made me feel better and called out to the intruder. "What are you doing in my aunt's house?" I tried to sound angry and authoritative. I only succeeded in sounding like a terrified child.

"It's been so long." The whisper became a long-drawn-out sigh. "Soooo long. I'm so tired of waiting. But you're here now, Lexi so my waiting is over."

I held my breath and tried to pinpoint the source of the whisper. In the room, perhaps, because it sounded close, but I could see nothing in the inky blackness as it whispered again. "Lexi Tremaine, you are perfect. You are what I want. Need. And will have."

Laughter followed, low and whispery and prolonged and evil. Definitely evil. "I stopped by to introduce myself but I'll let you go back to sleep. For now. But I'll be back. Now and then. But I'll let you alone until I'm ready." Then it continued. "Sweet dreams, Lexi." Followed by more whispery laughter that echoed from one wall to another and set my teeth on edge. "You have a while yet. A little while." The whisper finished with, "So, until next time, have a good night Lexiiii... Lexiii... Lexiii..." Then it was gone.

Sudden, stunning silence reigned and I somehow knew there'd be no more whispers because whoever was intruding in my life was gone. They felt gone, anyway. The cottage felt empty and, as I thought about it, I realized the night had felt different while the intruder was there. Darker. Oppressive. With a slight scent I couldn't recognize. Something burning? I was too upset to try to identify it.

But they'd succeeded in what they were clearly trying to do. To scare me. I was beyond terrified and, though I was sure they were done whispering and fairly sure they'd left and the night was once more just another spring night, there was a possibility they were still in the cottage. Hiding. Waiting. They could be still there.

So I forced myself to switch on the bedside lamp. The room was empty but that didn't mean the whisperer wasn't still nearby. He – and when I thought about it I knew it was a male voice, no doubt about that – could be in the kitchen or the alcove or anywhere at all.

I eyed the suitcase on the chair where I'd left it, being too tired to put anything in drawers. There was a twenty-two pistol in that suitcase mere yards away, one I'd bought for protection and taken classes to learn how to use it.

That time had come.

I rose, padded to the suitcase, pulled out the pistol and loaded it as I'd been taught. In a burst of unusual bravery on my part I told myself that whoever was in my aunt's house would be sorry they came if they were still nearby.

I approached the door to the rest of the cottage carefully, holding my weapon with two hands, also as I'd been taught, in order to better aim and fire quickly and accurately if someone was on the other side with the intent to do harm. And the voice had made it abundantly clear that was the plan.

But when I kicked the door open no one was there. Nor in the alcove. Nor the main room that made up most of the cottage. Soon the entire building was ablaze with light as I checked every corner of every room, turning on lights and leaving them on as I searched for the whisperer.

He wasn't there.

So where'd he come from and how'd he leave so quickly? I decided to check the locks on the doors. What I found made me suck in my breath and wonder what could be happening because the deadbolts were still in place and there was no evidence of tampering. I checked the windows next. They, too, were closed and securely locked as they'd been all winter with a layer of dust saying they'd not been disturbed. Even the window that had been broken was still covered with cardboard and tight against the night. So who had been in the cottage? How had they entered and how had they left?

I put the twenty-two on the kitchen table and made coffee, strong and black because I'd not sleep any more that night so I might as well have something to drink as

I waited for dawn and sanity. I sank onto a straight-backed kitchen chair and tried to rationalize what had happened.

Could it have been my imagination? A nightmare? Maybe my subconscious was telling me I shouldn't be trying to start my own business turning discarded things into objects of value. Perhaps I should have stayed in the city instead of coming to this cottage a few miles from a small town. An imaginary whisper in the night was the result.

I debated. As I stared at the twenty-two pistol on the table I came up with lots of reasons why it could have been a nightmare. But none of those things would cause nightmares as bad as I'd experienced. My current online marketing business brought in enough so the income from the new business would be extra and Aunt Gertrude had generously offered her cottage for free while she was in Europe. She'd said she'd have to pay utilities whether anyone was there or not so if I didn't go overboard on electric usage I didn't even need to worry about that.

So I wasn't concerned about my new endeavor. And I had no enemies.

So what had just happened? How had someone entered the cottage, whispered to me, and left without leaving a trace?

CHAPTER 2

I spent the rest of the night at the table in the brightly lit kitchen as if it was an island of safety in a sea of danger, ignoring that I needed sleep after days of travel. I would take a nap the next day when it was light out and an intruder would be reluctant to enter the cottage.

I spent those long, dark hours staring out the window towards the east and waiting for the sun to rise. I willed it to appear soon and be bright and cheerful. I needed its light to chase away what had surely been the worst experience of my life.

I dug into the bags of groceries I'd bought in the last town and found a chocolate cake and ate the whole thing while waiting for dawn while trying to convince myself that it must, indeed, have been a nightmare even though I knew it had been real.

But when dawn finally came and the sun rose high enough for the entire world to be light and the day birds to come out, I followed through on a plan I'd made while sitting at that kitchen table. I'd find out once and for all how the intruder had done what he'd done. Then I'd find him and let him know what I thought of people who tried to scare someone in the middle of the night. Perhaps I'd press charges. Yes, absolutely I would.

I went outside and circled the entire cottage looking for something – anything – that could send sounds into my bedroom without someone breaking the locks and actually entering the cottage. I looked for a speaker. A megaphone. An electric cord that might have been left by whoever had been there and plugged one end into a recording device and the other into a car battery. I found no device.

Then I looked for footprints or car treads in the grass though it hadn't rained so the ground was hard and I feared they might not show. I examined every inch of my aunt's yard carefully and surely would have seen something if someone had been there.

Nor did I see car tracks in the driveway other than mine from when I arrived. Since my car had made slight tracks it only made sense that if another car had been there too, there would be additional tire tracks. But there were none.

I decided to make doubly sure. The whispers had been so frightening I would do anything to find out what had happened. So I looked past the cottage on its postage stamp sized lakeshore lot. Could the whispers have come from one of the several other cottages scattered along the lakeshore?

I decided to check them out, grabbing a sweater against the coolness of the morning and driving slowly along the gravel road that followed the lakeshore with evenly spaced driveways leading to those neighboring cottages, some hidden by trees or undergrowth while others were easily seen perched next to the lake.

I stopped at each and every driveway and looked for evidence of human habitation. I found none. Several of the driveways were behind locked gates that looked like they'd been locked for months judging by the leaves and small branches that would have to be cleared before anyone could drive to the cottages they guarded.

I passed a man out for a morning run. I looked closer and recognized the gorgeous man who'd helped me break into my aunt's house. The man without a name. From the safety of my car I examined every inch of his muscular body with awe as we nodded briefly to each other.

He'd helped me once. I found myself irrationally wanting to stop, jump out of my car and ask for more help. Surely he could find the whisperer. He was definitely competent and would know what to do. But I didn't because he'd laugh and those blue eyes would ice up again and I'd freeze to death.

All of the cottages lined the gravel road that hugged the lake and went all the way to the tiny town where I'd gotten groceries the evening before. The chocolate cake. But on the other side of my aunt's cottage was a house. A real house, not a cottage, with two stories, a large garage, a medium sized shed, and an actual porch overlooking the lake instead of the more usual deck. But I didn't check it out because it was empty and falling down. It wasn't suitable for human habitation. No one could possibly live there.

It had been for sale forever and would probably never sell because making it livable would be a monumental task, never mind that the property was lovely, encompassing acres of woods as well as lakeshore with a swimming beach my aunt had always envied and the building itself sat on a good foundation and had what my aunt called 'good bones.' But it wasn't livable.

After returning from my examination of the cottages between my aunt's cottage and the nearby town, I paused and looked at the trees and tall bushes between my aunt's cottage and that falling-down house. The stretch of wilderness separating the house from my cottage was thicker and wilder than ever and visiting the house would require a bit of a walk and I was tired. So I decided to check it out some other time. Eventually I would go there to make sure I'd checked all possibilities. But not now.

Then I turned away from the thick underbrush and examined my aunt's cottage and told myself that I'd done enough sleuthing and had better start making the cottage my own and get started on my new business because the logical conclusion to my sleuthing was that the whisperer wasn't real. The whole thing had been a nightmare after all, never mind that it had been more realistic than any dream ever.

But before working, I'd spend a while admiring the lake and being grateful to have it in my life for the summer, thanks to Aunt Gertrude. I entered the cottage and went through to the back to the deck overlooking the lake. I removed the protective cover from one of the two lounge chairs on the deck, stuffed it into the storage bin that held everything anyone could want while outside enjoying the day, and dropped onto the lounge and stared at the lake, lazy blue and close to summer warm.

I lay back and tried to doze but couldn't. The sun rose high in the sky and then still higher until it brought enough warmth that I discarded my sweater, thinking summer was coming fast and I should stop obsessing over nightmares and admiring the water glittering like a million diamonds and get my new enterprise going or I'd never have the business I wanted.

I hadn't even unloaded the car, for goodness sake, and I'd never thought of myself as lazy so I'd best get going. So with great difficulty I tore my eyes from the riffles on the lake. But I didn't get busy and I didn't unload the car.

Instead I fell half asleep, lulled by the warming breeze and the birds trilling in the slice of forest between the cottage and the decrepit house next door and I spent the rest of the day in that lounge chair doing nothing except being glad I was there and had finally reconciled reality with nightmares and knew the whisperer wasn't real.

A day wasted? No, it had been a day spent in much needed relaxation and discerning the difference between reality and my imagination. Imagination won. I'd had a nightmare.

When evening came, though, since I hadn't actually slept previously, I was truly exhausted. Several nights with little to no sleep did that. I staggered into the cabin, forgot about dinner and practically fell into bed. I kicked my shoes off, punched the pillow into a semblance of comfort, pulled a blanket over me and fell into the kind of sleep I'd expected to experience the night before.

Didn't happen. As the previous night, I was awakened by a sound. A whisper.

"Lexi."

I didn't sit up this time. Instead I crawled deeper beneath the blankets and pulled the pillow over my head.

"Lexi Tremaine."

I shoved the pillow aside and looked around. I tried to wrap my mind around what was happening. I sat up deciding that this time I'd do something. I'd not just sit and let whoever it was scare me to death. So I spoke. Loudly. Bravely. "Who are you?"

The whispery voice laughed indulgently. "Dear, dear Lexi Tremaine. You are delightful. I enjoy you ever so much." The voice laughed again with a sinister undertone I'd not noticed before. Now it set my entire body thrumming with fear. "As I'll enjoy you when you are mine." The whisper went silent but only for a moment. "And you *will* be mine. No doubt about it." Then it faded but as it did it repeated my name over and over again. "Lexi … Lexi … Lexiiii …" drawing out my name until finally silence reigned.

I spent the rest of that night wrapped in blankets with my eyes open because I was afraid to fall asleep. I watched dawn creep along the shore and reach the cottage and bring with it a semblance of peace. I should get up. Now the whispers had happened two night in a row, I knew they were real. Not a nightmare. Not a dream.

Then, as the sun came fully awake, something else happened. I heard a sound.

Not the whisper. This sound was completely different. It was a very real voice coming through the air from somewhere not far away. It was loud and boisterous and clearly male and singing a song that was totally off tune and completely, riotously cheerful and happy.

After a night filled with terror I needed happiness and that song gave it to me.

It went straight to my core. It gave me happiness on a silver platter of joy that pushed aside the night and the whisperer. So I sat up, still wrapped in my comforter and greedily took in every scrap of happiness the singer sent my way.

Who was singing? The nearby cottages were empty and I doubted anyone had moved in while I was sleeping. So who was it? And where did the singing come from?

I padded to the sliding door that opened onto the lakeside deck and stepped out to hear better and realized that the house next door, the one on the other side of that green jungle of trees and brush, the one that was a falling down wreck, must be occupied after all because there was no doubt that was where the sound originated.

My first thought was that I wasn't alone and that thought made me realize how frightened the whisperer had made me. But the song meant things were different now. I had a neighbor and he sounded like a nice guy. He sounded like someone who loved life and the glorious day that was beginning as the sun rose bright in the sky and he unknowingly was sharing his happiness with the world through his songs, even though he couldn't carry a tune in a bushel basket.

I found myself smiling and impulsively started towards the happy sound. Then I stopped because I wasn't ready to meet him. Not yet. My hair was a mess and my clothes were wrinkled from being stuffed in suitcases. I should wait until I was presentable before making the trek around the forest between our places and introducing myself.

In the bathroom I looked at myself in the mirror. Yuck. My hair was a mess and my lack of sleep showed. My eyes were shadowed. My hair was long, to my waist because long hair was uncomplicated and easy to maintain, few haircuts, but every inch of that hair now looked pretty much like the jungle between the house and my aunt's cottage and it would take a long time to untangle it, not to mention that it hadn't been washed since before leaving home and was an ugly, dirty brown instead of just brown. And of course, if I hadn't washed my hair, neither had I washed the rest of me. In short, I was a disaster. No visit today.

CHAPTER 3

I'd meet my new neighbor tomorrow. But as I scrubbed my face in a futile attempt to scrub away shadows and washed all of me, especially my hair and brushed it into a semblance of normalcy and finally toweled off, clean and dry, I kept thinking about the awful, off-tune happy songs and was glad to have heard each and every one.

I went about my day with every window open to hear better. I listened to the singer's next song and the one after that and then still more as morning and then afternoon wore on.

I wondered what my neighbor was like and what the house that had been falling down for so many years would be like and decided it would be beautiful. Of course it would be. Anyone who loved singing as he did would also love beauty

A lot must have been accomplished in the past year. Construction crews. Builders. Painters. Gardeners. And more. I found myself looking forward to whatever transformation had taken place and to getting to know the new owner and I went to bed that night smiling and thinking about the house next door and the unknown man who lived there. The singer.

But I didn't sleep. Of course I didn't.

As I heard the now familiar sibilant hissing come through the night, I finally accepted that wherever the whispers originated wasn't the real world. That knowledge – that awareness -- had been building in my subconscious since that first night and somehow, for some unknown reason, that night solidified the knowing. Where it came from I couldn't know. But I knew it to be true. The whisperer wasn't alive. He couldn't be. But he was somehow real.

Could something that wasn't alive hurt me? I hoped not. I tried to ignore the whispers and possibly because I never spoke they didn't last as long as the other nights and when they finally ended I managed to get enough sleep to actually get some rest. Not much, but some.

The next morning I took a long shower and rinsed my face with cold water to wake me up until, staring into the bathroom mirror I decided I looked better than the day before. I was almost normal. It was time to meet my neighbor.

There were no raucous, happy songs, not yet, but it was early and just knowing someone was nearby made me feel better. He didn't have to sing all the time, just often enough for me to know I wasn't alone and for me to steal some of the happiness those songs scattered about so freely.

I grabbed a quick breakfast, pulled a brush through my too-long hair and managed to untangle it for the third time that morning, checked myself for the hundredth time in the mirror and then I went out the sliding glass doors to the deck overlooking the lake and from there to the beach, slogging through the sand barefoot even though it was cold. I walked past the thick forest between my aunt's cottage and the house next door.

I looked to see what had been done to the disaster of a place. And stopped in stunned surprise.

Not because it was suddenly transformed into a showplace. It wasn't. It was pretty much as I remembered from past years except the worst of the mess had been torn away and was now in a dumpster beside a tent erected in the yard with a very large table in front of it.

There were things in the yard that spoke of construction. A pile of fresh, new-smelling lumber. Boxes of what I guessed to be hardware of various types though it was hard to tell because they were covered against the weather by tarps that were staked to the ground. Roof shingles, light gray in color, were far enough to one side that they most likely weren't to be used soon. And so on.

Clearly the construction was barely begun which meant the singing I'd heard was by one of the construction workers instead of the owner, though what purpose the tent served I couldn't imagine. An office, perhaps, because of the table in front, though there wasn't any business equipment on the table.

I took a few steps closer to see what was on it and was rewarded by the sight of a coffee mug and a thermos jug, plus a plastic box containing donuts. Yep, it belonged to the construction crew.

I was curious to see more of the remodel while knowing it was wrong to trespass. But curiosity got the better of me and I went to the house anyway to see what was being done. I stepped through the doorway that no longer had a door and into the interior of a house that had been gutted to its bare bones. Only the exterior walls, a few interior ones, and the floors remained intact and in places even those walls were open to the weather. I could see lapping waves on the beach through window frames that no longer had windows in them, being mere rectangular spaces in the walls.

I looked closer. Some of the walls – the ones facing the lake – had chalk lines drawn on them. I tipped my head in thought until it came to me that they represented places where large windows would replace the smaller ones that had been there. The new ones would give a gorgeous view of my favorite lake. I liked whomever had insisted on those views without having met him. Or her. Or them. The new owners, whoever they were.

As I considered the chalk lines designating where new, huge windows would go I realized that several were placed for perfect viewing of the wilderness beside the house, the area between my aunt's cottage and this house. Because they wanted to watch wildlife up close as well as the beautiful lake.

Having seen what I could, I returned to the beach and then headed back to my aunt's cottage, toes once more digging deep in the cold sand.

If the new owners weren't happy people, I decided, it didn't truly matter because the remodel would surely take at least the entire summer, if not longer, so for the entire time I'd be living in the cottage I'd have the company of the cheerful construction crew and those happy, cheerful, off-key songs. Which meant it would be a good summer.

I danced in the sand as I made my way back to my cottage because I just knew the sounds of happy songs would chase away the whispers in the night. Starting tonight.

I'd introduce myself to the construction crew as soon as possible and let them know I liked music. Maybe I'd bring donuts.

Then I heard a sound. It came from the thicket between the cottage and the house under construction. I stopped, unsure whether to run as fast as possible or stand my ground to intimidate what must surely be some large, dangerous animal. The trees and bushes could hide anything.

I raised my arms as people are told to do when confronted with a large, dangerous animal because it would make me look larger than I am and more dangerous. I huffed and puffed and waited to see what would emerge from what I now considered a dangerous though rather small forest.

A woof came to me as a puppy, black and white and cute, meandered out of the trees and came towards me. It rubbed itself against my ankles and I deflated. My attacker wasn't dangerous after all. He was cute and friendly and wanted to be picked up and was a 'he.' That was obvious after a quick peek at his underside.

Where did he come from? The obvious answer was the house under construction because he surely didn't belong to any of the empty cottages along the lakeshore. One of the workers had a puppy.

"What's your name?" I asked and he answered by rubbing against my legs still more, asking for love and attention. "I'd love a four-legged visitor every so often and I'm here for the summer."

The puppy responded by following me to my cottage and into the main room where I found some leftover food that would work for treats and he knew exactly what I was doing which meant he was used to being pampered.

"Now what?" I went onto the deck and he followed. I sank into one of the lounge chairs and he climbed onto my lap and looked at me with the sure expectation of tummy rubs and more love, which I gave because my life lately had been horrible and puppy love felt right.

I pampered him for a long time. But eventually I had to get some work done so I dumped him off my lap and headed for my car to finally – finally – unload it and get started on that new business I was hoping would become profitable enough for me to make a living at it and I'd better get started or it would never earn a dime.

The puppy followed and then followed still more as I made trips back and forth between the car and the cottage and kept me company for a while. But as it became evident I was going to work instead of pampering him any longer he bid me farewell and disappeared back to the forest between my cottage and the house under construction.

I finished emptying my car, load after load until the car was bare and the cottage was full of boxes and bags and miscellaneous things strewn about because some of the things I'd brought just didn't fit into neat containers. And looked like trash. Because it was trash.

It was the stuff I'd got by dumpster diving for things to repurpose into useful and/or beautiful things that I could sell in person and online for enough money to support myself.

CHAPTER 4

I spent the rest of that day stowing things in corners and on tables and behind doors until I could at least walk through the cottage without tripping over some piece of junk that would become something beautiful once I'd figured out what it would become and had actually done the repurposing.

I broke for lunch but went back to work immediately after cleaning up after myself. I heard the singing again and smiled, thinking of the singer and the puppy having a good time together but I didn't go around the thicket between our houses because now I'd finally gotten started I wanted to get my own house in order so I could get my new business going as soon as possible.

After I was done unloading, a trip to the nearby small town was next on my to-do list for more dumpster diving and to see if there were stores where I could sell my finished items. Tomorrow, I decided, I'd go tomorrow after visiting my new neighbor.

It was a tourist town, I knew that much, so figured there'd be stores selling lovely items, both useless and useful, to visitors that would remind them of their special time there. Hopefully, some of those items would be mine.

I sighed in contentment just thinking about the future opening before me. And also because the singing next door was so happy that it made me happy and the thought of possible visits from a cute, friendly black and white puppy made my smile even broader.

After a productive day I ate dinner on the deck watching the sun set over the water and the stars come out bright and clean. I stayed up late because it was a lovely night even though it was still early enough in the season that I retrieved a blanket from the bedroom and wrapped myself in it to keep warm as I took in the night sights and sounds.

I only went to bed when I started nodding off. I didn't want to sleep on the deck and wake up in the morning with a crick in my neck because I had a full day ahead that involved finding both more junk to turn into beautiful items and a place to sell some of them. That would be in the afternoon, of course, after I met the construction crew in the morning. Especially the singer of happy songs who surely was also the owner of the puppy.

When I couldn't stay awake one second longer I dragged the blanket after me into the bedroom and locked the sliding glass doors securely because the whispers had made me overly conscious of being alone and it just seemed like a reasonable precaution in spite of the fact that I was in a laid-back rural area where crime was unknown and I'd had the glass replaced in the window that has been broken. And the locks changed, of course.

I didn't expect any whispers that night. They no longer held a spell over me and would never repeat.

Puppy love and happy, off-key songs and the smell of new wood had chased them away forever.

About that, I was wrong.

"Lexi."

I came awake, stomach heaving because how could it happen again after such a perfect day? "Who are you?" I screamed into the night, past fear, past anything except pure, unadulterated anger. I screamed again. "Leave me alone or I'll call the cops."

Laughter. Whispered laughter. "I so enjoy you, Lexi. Your sense of humor. Your useless threats."

"You're not real!" I screamed louder if such was possible, unsure whether I was glad the windows were shut so my screams wouldn't wake anyone who might be passing by and decide a demented person lived in the cottage. "You can't do anything because you're not real!"

More laughter echoed from wall to wall, whispered laughter but it came clearly through the inky black of the night. "Oh, I'm real, Lexi. I'm very ancient and very, very real."

"Leave me alone!" By then I didn't know if I was screaming or sobbing or both. I threw my pillow against the wall, hoping against hope I'd hit something. A shadow. A ghost. Anything, real or not. "I'm not afraid of you."

This time the laughter lasted for almost a minute. "Yes you are afraid of me, Lexi. You're very afraid and you're going to grow more and more afraid over time and that's exactly what I want."

"I'm not afraid and I'll laugh louder each time you bother me."

"No you won't, Lexi. I know you so I know you

are afraid – terrified – and each time I come your fear will grow until it consumes you. And weakens you."

"It won't!"

The whisper clucked softly. "And when the process is complete – when every cell in your body is afraid and weak and can't fight any longer – then you will belong to me. Totally. Completely. Every cell in your body, every thought in your head, every shard of your soul."

I threw the second pillow at the opposite wall and the same thing happened as when I threw the first one. Nothing. Absolutely nothing.

Except fear. Fear happened because I knew with a primitive kind of bone-deep knowledge that something both real and completely evil was behind the whisper. And it wanted me. I knew with that same bone-deep knowledge that if I couldn't figure how to stop it, it would have me. And eventually own me. All of me.

I got out of bed, turned on the light, pulled that twenty-two from where I'd decided it belonged, in the bedside table, and flashed it about in a melodramatic but useless gesture.

"Tut tut, Lexi, Bullets can't hurt me. They'll merely put holes in your aunt's walls and you'd have to explain why you shot up her cottage and chances are she'll call the nearest insane asylum and then every chance you might have of defeating me will be gone because such places are where I do my best work."

I put the pistol back in the shallow drawer and slammed it shut as I thought about what the whisperer had just said. I replayed the actual words. It had just said I had a chance to defeat it. Just a chance. But I'd take it. "I don't need a pistol. I will simply ignore you until you crawl back to wherever you came from like the scum you are."

"Lexiiii, Lexiiii, Lexiiii."

I'd already figured out that when he drew my name out like that and said it slowly it meant he was taking his leave. "See you later, Lexiiii. Sweet Lexiiii. My Lexiiii."

Then the whisper was gone and silence came as swiftly and completely as if nothing had happened. I sat up in bed, wide awake, pulled my knees to my chin and waited for dawn and the hope that comes with every new day as I prayed with every fiber of my being for that construction worker to be next door singing because I desperately needed his songs.

The sun came up as it always does and I crawled out of bed and padded to the bathroom. In the mirror I looked somewhat normal. Not completely normal but better than those first days.

Then something wonderful happened. I heard singing. Loud, boisterous, happy and totally off-key. It seemed so close I wondered if the singer was on the deck and had come for a visit, so I turned to look but it was empty.

When I turned back to the mirror, however, the shadows were disappearing, vanquished by my unknown singer. I smiled at my reflection and thanked whoever sang so badly for giving me the strength to face the day.

I didn't even pull a brush through my tangled mess of hair because I was in that much of a hurry to meet him. I forgot to wear shoes, dashing along the cold early spring sand and not noticing as I ran beside the jungle of trees and bushes that pretty much resembled my hair. A mess.

I stopped before reaching my neighbor's yard. Moved close to the thick forest and hid behind a tree. And slowly, cautiously, as sneakily as possible, peered around it to inspect the construction crew and identify the singer.

My mouth dropped open in surprise. And shock. Because there was no crew. Instead, there was just one man carrying a dozen or more new two-by-fours from a pile on the edge of the yard towards the house.

One man. Not a crew. But it was the identity of that single man that made me stand without moving. Without thinking. With my mouth open.

Because that one lone man was the man who'd rescued me when I fell off a pile of suitcases. My savior who'd gotten me safely inside the cottage. That man was also the man who sang the songs that drifted on the air and reached me and reminded me the world was a good place. Totally off-key songs sung by a man whose smile turned the world so bright that the smile alone could surely – surely – chase an evil whisperer away and defeat any enemy.

I took a deep breath and stepped from behind the tree and walked towards him to introduce myself and I forgot how to breathe when he turned and noticed me.

He stopped carrying those two-by-fours and dropped them carefully to the ground and we stood there without speaking for the longest time, staring at each other over those two-by-fours in the heat of the day with a black and white puppy running between us.

Then he smiled even wider and, yes, it was that same thousand-watt smile increased by a power of ten and I knew – just knew – that no whisperer in the night could ever frighten this man and I wondered how I could get him to stay with me the next time I was afraid.

He nodded. He remembered me. And came towards me with a ground-eating stride that spoke of male confidence and lots of hard physical work.

"Hi." That one word, in a deep baritone that matched the singer's and sent a thrill through my entire body, asked a question. "Are you okay? Do you need something?" As if I'd known who he was all along and had come for help as neighbors are wont to do.

I stepped closer as if pulled by a magnet. We met in the middle of the yard surrounded by construction debris and grass just turning green as the puppy of the previous day jumped against my leg. I stooped to pet him. "Hello, there, puppy. How are you today?"

"Uh oh." The man whistled and the puppy went to him and was lifted up and held, a squirming, black and white mass of fur. "Shame on you. Bothering the nice lady." He turned from the puppy to me. "Has he been visiting? Bothering you?" An apology was in his voice.

"What? The puppy? Bothering me? No! Of course not. He's cute. We met the other day and he visited me for a while, but he wasn't a bother." I finished with, "We're friends."

Relief showed and my new neighbor let the squirming puppy fall back to the ground where he continued his circling of the two of us. "Good. I was kind of worried when I realized someone was moving in next door. I love him but he can be a pest." He was the kind of man who could admit to loving a puppy without being embarrassed. My estimation of my neighbor soared straight into the atmosphere.

Then he realized what I'd said. "He visited you?"

He looked at the puppy and frowned. "He knows he's not supposed to wander. He could get lost."

I shook my head. "He didn't wander. I came to introduce myself and he followed me home. He's a good puppy. We became friends. I hope you let him visit again." I took a deep breath. "I'm Lexi Tremain. Your next door neighbor and I now use a door instead of a window to get in my aunt's cottage."

"I'm Zackary – Zack -- and I didn't expect anyone yet. It's early for summer people." He pretended to shudder. "It's still cold." He looked at the lake a few yards away with small waves lapping across the sand. "Especially the lake. It's really cold."

"I'm not summer people."

His head tipped as the small puppy came to me and said he needed to be picked up. So I did and the tall, dark and handsome guy in front of me watched with approval. Then he tipped his head towards the table that still held one cup and a thermos of something and led the way across the yard. Now I knew why there was only one cup on that table. Because there was only one man working on the house.

Miraculously, though, a second cup appeared from somewhere along with another chair and soon we had coffee and donuts as the puppy continued to run circles around us. "His name is Little Guy because that's what he is."

His face turned kind of red and he tried to hide behind his coffee cup as he realized how that sounded. "I know. No one names a dog Little Guy, especially if it's a mutt and might grow up to be huge."

"Evidently someone does and that someone is you." He'd come up with an impromptu name for his puppy that somehow was just right. And he was obviously remodeling an old house by himself. And he sang happy songs in a voice most people would laugh at.

Should I tell him how much those songs meant to me? I couldn't. He'd think I was being snarky. So I just drank coffee and chatted and was glad we met and were talking. I was surprised at myself because I'm an introvert but I didn't feel like one at the moment.

I decided to be conversational. "What's with the remodel?" I can be diplomatic when the occasion requires diplomacy. "It's a huge job."

He turned and inspected the house. The areas where rotten wood had been removed, the chalk rectangles I knew were inside to mark where huge windows would go. The whole thing. "It's big, I admit that. But it's mine."

Pride of ownership was clear as he chuckled. "It's what I could afford. But by the time it's too hot to sleep in my tent comfortably the house will be closed to the weather and will have plumbing and electric and air conditioning and everything and I'll move in." He paused. "It won't be finished, of course, but it'll be livable and that's all I need for the foreseeable future."

We were having a conversation. I searched for the kind of topic people who'd just met might discuss because I wanted this moment to last as long as possible. "Did you move here recently?"

"Just got out of the Army and this is my piece of heaven and I moved so many times in the service that I'm never going to move again. Ever."

I examined the piles of wood, hardware and other things that went with building a house. "Are you doing this all by yourself?"

"Yep." The pride in his voice said how he felt about the decrepit house that eventually would be a showplace.

I tried not to notice muscles that rippled along his arms and thighs and all of him that suddenly made sense with such a formidable task ahead of him. "It looks like a lot of work."

He leaned back and inspected me. Up and down and sidewise. And smiled. "I suppose so. Maybe." A chuckle was followed by, "I don't want to freeze my tush off this winter so I'm highly motivated to get it closed in and at least basically livable before cold weather sets in."

I didn't know what I was going to say next until the words came out. "You'll do it. I have no doubt." And I didn't. Not with that ripped body and enthusiasm that fizzed through his body like champagne.

Then guilt swept over me. "Am I keeping you from your work?"

Those eyes inspected me a second time, taking in every atom of my being. I felt myself thrumming wherever those eyes lit for even a second. I thought he approved of what he saw though it was hard to tell.

"Naaaah. Everyone needs a break now and then."

He let that ripped body relax, unfolding one muscle at a time. "It's my house. My job. My schedule. I can take a break whenever I want, which is one of the benefits of not being in the military any longer. My time is my own."

He shaded his eyes with one hand and chuckled still again as he examined the house closer. "To a point, anyway. I do have to get some stuff done because it's a mess, isn't it?" I had to agree, my face turning red because it wasn't polite to say something was a mess but it would be dishonest to say otherwise as he simply added, "It's okay. I knew what I was buying when I signed on the dotted line."

"Why not buy something new?" Though in an upscale resort area, nothing was cheap.

He tipped his head. "Because this was what I wanted." He swept an arm to take in the entirety of the property. "Acres of land. A tiny forest that almost touches the house. And the most beautiful lake imaginable just beyond my front door."

He stuck out those long legs that had enabled him to break my aunt's window by merely reaching up and bashing in the glass and he clasped his hands behind his head. "It's perfection. Or will be when I'm done." He shrugged. "And in the meantime, it's summer, it's getting warmer by the day, and how exactly are you not summer people?" Returning to my original statement that I wasn't exactly summer people.

I explained about living in my aunt's cottage while getting my new business going. His eyes showed surprise but I thought he was pleased with the idea. "You're like me, then. Starting a new life. A new business."

"What's your business?" A store in town, perhaps? A physical fitness gym? Something more ambitious?

"I'm going to become a handyman." I blinked and he shrugged. "I know. It's not the most glamorous profession but I have some money saved from my time in the Army plus a pension and there's no mortgage on the house so my bills are relatively few and a handyman business lets me choose my own hours. That's a big plus after having been told when to rise, when to go to bed, and what to do during all the hours in between."

"When you put it like that, it's sounds great."

"So what are you doing?" He inspected me again. Up and down, side to side as the first time, only this look took me apart inside and out. "Let me guess. You're a computer nerd and it's something online."

It was my turn to grin. "I was a computer nerd. Past tense. I'm trying to get out of the nerd business." I explained about dumpster diving for things that I could upcycle into items people would buy.

"You mean people will actually pay money for junk someone else threw away?"

"It won't be junk by the time I'm done with it. It'll be wonderful. Or I hope it will be." I explained that I'd done my homework, on a computer of course, and that I already had a marketing business so I knew how to maximize my sales potential.

"Really? That's an actual thing? Maximizing sales potential?"

I turned red and agreed that it was, indeed, a thing and suddenly we were laughing. Not uproariously but the day was beautiful, the sky was filled with fuzzy, white clouds and I'd forgotten completely that some evil thing was scaring the crap out of me at night.

I decided after covertly examining the gorgeous and very physically fit man before me who obviously had never been afraid of anything in his entire life that I'd not tell him about the whispers.

Because sitting there watching confidence ooze from his every pore and feeling that confidence reach out to me on the other side of the table and wrap me in the overflowing optimism he seemed to specialize in –

well, what with that zinging through my body, the whole whisperer thing suddenly seemed ridiculous. It wouldn't happen again. It couldn't, not after such a perfect day.

CHAPTER 5

Before I rose from the table and we went our separate ways, Zack apologized for singing. He actually apologized for the thing that was keeping me sane. "I know my singing isn't the best." He rubbed the back of his neck and tried to hide the faint red flushing his face. "It's just the loudest. But I promise I won't bother you again. I'll stop singing. I didn't know ..."

He was about to tell me he hadn't known the cottage was occupied but I stopped him before he could finish. I actually reached over the table and placed two fingers on his lips to shush him and I'm not the type to do something like that. Something so bold. Never. Ever. Not me. But I did that day because what I was about to say was important. "Please don't stop. I love your singing."

As my fingers left his lips those lips made a round 'O' of surprise. "Huh? You actually like my not very good yodeling because I'm sure it should never be called actual singing. Maybe not even yodeling. Maybe I'm an insult to yodelers."

I was feeling brave because sitting there his bravery had rubbed off on me, so I easily spoke the truth as I relapsed back into my chair and stared him down. Actually stared. Met him look for look because I needed him to know how much I wanted him to continue singing. "I love your off-key yodeling if that's what it is though I consider it music."

I was too cowardly to tell him how badly I needed it. He didn't need to know the details, didn't need to know what an emotional wreck sat across the table. Just that I wanted him to continue.

His face turned deeply red and he kind of slumped lower in a feeble attempt to hide his embarrassment because of course he didn't believe me. I was just being polite. The red face that said the perfect male across the table from me had an imperfection. He was capable of being embarrassed. I loved that imperfection. I felt empowered by it.

I leaned over the table until we were mere inches apart. "I love it when you sing. I truly love it." He thought I was just continuing to be polite until he read the sincerity in my face. In my word as I finished with, "Don't stop singing. Ever." And I added, "Please."

That did it. He believed me though it was clear he thought I must be tone deaf as he shrugged and I moved even closer and stared straight into those eyes that were no longer ice blue but rather the color of the sky above the lake in my eagerness to make sure he understood I wanted him to continue singing. After still another examination of me up, down and sidewise followed by a puzzled expression, he said simply, "Okay."

The single word came out in a rush as our looks interlocked, his wondering if I was insane and mine making sure he understood that I wanted to hear every song, off key and as loud as possible. He tipped his head uncertainly. Did he think he lived next door to a crazy woman? "If you're sure …"

"I'm sure."

I didn't know if what happened next was my imagination coupled with my incredible need for whatever it was about him that spread confidence over everything but especially over me, or if it was perhaps some accidental thing that happened as our eyes met momentarily. I didn't know if the connection between us was real or imaginary. But there was a connection. At least I chose to believe we connected and that the connection was at some truly deep level I'd not known existed until then.

It was weird as we sat there and stared at each other. Okay it was just a feeling and feelings aren't always accurate. Still it felt stronger and deeper than I'd have believed possible and I didn't know how to handle it. I just knew that the man across the table from me had changed some fundamental thing in me and, yes, I knew that was impossible but I also knew it had happened.

I didn't know if it was something new and wonderful that was beginning or whether it was just momentary. Just that it was real. At least it was real to me.

But he felt it too, I saw the knowledge in his eyes, flared and bluer than blue, and he was just as uncomfortable about what was happening between us as I was. So we just sat there for a long time and stared at each other as Little Guy circled us and jumped at our bodies and barked for attention.

Then the moment passed. Zack's eyes narrowed and I easily read his thoughts though I hadn't been able to do so before that strange moment when our souls had met, if that's what had happened and I thought that's what it must have been.

But it had been more than that. His eyes said that during that shared moment he'd figured out that there was something I wasn't telling him. He'd seen deep enough inside me to know there was something else. Something more. Something negative.

Knit brows wondered what the unknown thing was. The thing he saw in my eyes as we'd connected in that man-woman way I'd never experienced with anyone else. But he merely nodded when I rose and said I had things to do and had best be going home.

I felt him staring after me as I passed the mini forest and strode barefoot once more along the sandy beach that wasn't quite as cold as when I'd come because the sun was doing its work and turning a cold lake into a warm and welcoming summer tourist destination and the sand into something to dig ones toes into.

I sent up sprays of sand as I ran from those questioning eyes, ignoring how badly I wanted to stand still and luxuriate in what they were saying. That I was a woman, an interesting woman, a woman he wanted to get to know better. Albeit one with a secret.

I managed to get nothing done the rest of that morning and had a quick lunch of a can of salmon in a can of cream of mushroom soup over a piece of toast. I'm a foodie and it wasn't my best culinary creation but I wasn't in the mood to do the work of a great lunch. Zack – I could now put a name to the man who'd kept me sane -- had that effect on me. Cream of mushroom soup, for goodness sake. The staple of lazy cooks and I'd used it with no feeling of guilt whatsoever.

After lunch I decided to head to town. I'd reconnoiter places to sell my future treasures and maybe get a bit of dumpster diving done, it being something I'd be doing a lot of if I wanted to find enough junk to turn into someone else's treasures.

So I set off in my car and parked on the main street of the town. Lewistown, it was called, after the lake and both were named after someone who had lived so long ago that no one remembered anything about him.

It was a small town but large enough that the streets were paved. There were several side streets and there was a stop light at the only semi-busy intersection. It was practically empty in winter and overflowing with people in the summer. And summer was coming fast.

Most of the tourist stores weren't open yet, but the café beside the lake catered to those few people there all year and had outdoor tables though no one was occupying them. It was too cold but, as I wondered what to do, I realized the sun had enough heat in it that if there was no breeze it felt like summer and warmed the area to spring warm but not summer hot. I looked at those outdoor tables and wished I'd not had cream of mushroom soup with salmon on toast for lunch. The café probably had a dozen better dishes.

"Want coffee and dessert? My treat."

Pleasant shivers moved up and down my spine as I looked for the speaker and recognized my neighbor. Zack Slater. The most gorgeous man I'd ever seen and, in a moment of absolute honesty, I admitted he was also the guy I was already in lust with. Totally. Completely. I cleared my throat and managed to speak normally. "Sure."

"Want to have it outside? It's beautiful out here but

you might get chilly." He wouldn't get cold, that body could obviously take anything nature could throw at it, but he was thinking of me. A fragile female. I pointed to the sweater I'd tied to my waist and he nodded that I could handle a little cool weather.

"Let's go inside and see what they have."

I followed him and soon we were outside with cappuccino and slices of peach pie, the gourmet dessert I needed that I could devour with ecstasy as I stared over it at the man of my dreams. I could sit there forever and simply feast on both the pie and the man. Except it's rude to stare so I found myself looking anywhere but at him as I sipped cappuccino and ate my pie slowly, as good manners dictated and because it extended our time together.

Then I realized he was doing the same. Trying not to look directly at me while turning to me frequently and then away quickly if our eyes met. Sipping slowly and eating sparingly just like me but I was sure a man of his size and physical prowess usually ate like a horse. Had to or he'd starve.

I'd figured he might be interested in me when we'd met at his house. Because of that moment between us that I couldn't explain. But I hadn't been positive because attraction is a subtle thing. But now? Meeting a second time? Was it man-woman attraction?

I thought so. I was almost sure. But how to find out for sure without looking like a predatory female? I hadn't a clue what the next step should be and as we stared at each other over peach pie and cappuccino, clearly, neither did he though I was fairly certain he wanted to take things between us further.

So we talked about nothing in particular and ate

our dessert as slowly as possible and ignored the electricity that sparked between us every time our looks connected. I wondered if the few people strolling along the sidewalks thought lightning was striking. But no one paid any attention to us so maybe it was just between us.

Most of all, as I surreptitiously examined the man across the table from me I felt like celebrating because there was definitely something happening between us. Something real. Hopefully emotional.

Zack cleared his throat. Because he was having just as hard a time speaking as I was? "I'm running errands. Getting more lumber. I can't believe how much lumber it's taking to get that house of mine livable. What are you doing in town?"

"I'm looking for places to sell my upscaled junk and maybe I'll get a little dumpster diving done."

He blinked. Knitted his brows in an effort to figure out what I was talking about. Grinned widely when he did. "Want some help? I can haul you out of the dumpsters when you get yourself in too deep."

I laughed and suddenly was comfortable instead of so stressed by the lust thing I couldn't function. "Sure."

He looked around. Read the sign on the store next to the café. It wasn't open but it was an art and craft gallery. A magnet for tourists. "Looks like a good place to sell your stuff."

"I should talk to the owner. He might have space for my stuff."

"Never hurts to ask. I'll carry some of your stuff if it's heavy and I'll give him a nasty stare if doesn't want it."

I giggled. I actually giggled and I hadn't done that

since middle school. And instead of giving me a look of distain at the childish sound he just grinned widely and repeated his offer so I'd know he meant it and hadn't just been making conversations. "We neighbors need to stick together."

His words almost knocked me sidewise. He was my neighbor and that reminded me of what happened every night in the cottage next to his house. Could I count on him if the whisperer came again?

Probably not. That wasn't what he'd been talking about because he didn't know about the whisperer and whispers in the night were beyond any kind of usual neighborhood helpfulness though I wished with all my heart that I could call on him if the whisperer returned.

But I simply said I'd appreciate his help if it was ever needed and explained about dumpster diving because that was the present concern. "Plastic bags is the biggest thing. I need lots of them."

"They are light weight. You don't need my help with them."

"And furniture, eventually, to refinish and refurbish and turn into something else."

"That'll be heavy."

I nodded and imagined the two of us working together. Those muscles lifting heavy things while I watched in awe and pretended not to notice, not to mention that the help would be appreciated. "I'll repay you." I looked straight at him. "I'll help with your house."

His eyes went wide. "I never thought about help. I figured I'd do everything myself."

"Why?"

"Because it's cheaper. I have enough money for

everything if I don't hire anyone."

"It'll be an exchange of work. No money involved."

He considered. "It might work."

"It will work."

And we were smiling at each other like a couple of idiots and somehow we finished our cappuccino and peach pie in spite of the smiling and dawdling and trying to make it last as long as possible. Then we went to finish his errands and do some dumpster diving. Together.

My toes curled and neither of us could stop smiling as we exited the café and headed for the lumber yard with his hand on my lower back gently moving me in the right direction and sending me into spasms of happiness.

CHAPTER 6

Two hours later we were ready to return to our respective homes. Zack had a truck full of building supplies and I had a car full of junk with the potential to become lovely objects to sell. With his help, of course, because, as he'd suspected, I'd have become a piece of trash myself doomed to live the rest of my life in a dumpster if he hadn't been there to pull me out.

He was grinning the whole time though he was too polite to say what he was thinking. Of course I knew exactly what he was thinking because his expression was a giveaway. That I was one truly odd woman who actually climbed into dumpsters. Oh well, it was in a good cause, that cause being my future business with enough income to keep the lights on. He, of course, didn't have to do weird things to get his house completed. Lumber isn't junk.

He looked down at me. "Want another cappuccino after all our exertions? That is, if they'll let us in their establishment after dumpster diving?"

I stuck my nose in the air and ignored his grin. "I do not stink, I'll have you know. I was very careful when in those dumpsters. I always am." I wasn't about to tell him I was careful ever since experiencing a mishap in one dumpster that hadn't been emptied in a long time and having to bathe for about an hour afterwards. He didn't need to know that. "Besides, we can have our drinks at the outside tables. Along with more pie. Apple, I think, this time. I love apple pie."

So we adjourned to the café once more and carried our cappuccinos and pie outside and found a table in the warm sun that a few weeks later would be too hot. But that day our greedy bodies absorbed the rays happily.

Zack leaned back comfortably. Looked around. Took in the signs over the businesses that lined the main street. Looked for a long time at the sign on the store next to the café. It wasn't open yet but looked like someone had been inside cleaning and arranging, getting ready for the tourist influx soon to come. "Should we check it out?"

I followed his look. Arthur Artworks. "I wonder what they sell, exactly. High end art for rich people who don't have any artistic knowledge so only buy from places that promise their items will be acceptable by any art critic?"

"Or is it a store that sells art and also stuff normal people buy?"

"I should find out."

When we finished with our cappuccinos and pies and returned our dirty dishes to the café, we wandered over to the store. That was when we saw the smaller sign in the window. 'High end art and crafts for everyone."

I tried the door. It was locked.

"Let's go around to the back. If someone is inside the back door might be unlocked because that's what they are using."

We went around the building and found a back door but it was locked and the parking space for the owner's car was empty. "I wonder when he's here."

We asked the café owner. "Most days he's here in the afternoons. He must be otherwise occupied today." Because it was already afternoon. "But try him another day." She looked at us. Then at me because I was obviously the crafter. "What's your name? I'll tell him you're interested."

I gave her my name and phone number. Not that he'd call but it never hurt. And then we went home in our respective vehicles and we each unloaded our treasures. He quickly, I was sure, while singing those loud, raucous, off-key songs and me slowly while enjoying every song he sang, taking in the safety and happiness of what might be considered music. Most of all I thought about the man who sang them. They were my future protection against the night whisperer.

Soon the lake would be warm enough to swim in. Even now if someone was used to arctic waters they'd go for a swim. Not me, but some brave souls. And when it was a bit warmer the lake would be filled with swimmers and boats and all sorts of water-based activities and people doing all kinds of things that got them wet. And I'd join them and not give the whisperer a second thought.

There were hours left in the day. Enough time stretched ahead that I could find a spot for my computer in the alcove and turn it into my office. I needed an office if I was to have a functioning business and soon I was hard at work creating a website for my new business and going crazy trying to think of a name for it because, of course, I needed a name to put in brightly blazing letters across the top of my website. What to call it?

I sat back and closed my eyes. And listened to those off-key songs coming through the tiny forest between our homes and then through the open windows of my cottage. And I knew the name had to have something to do with those songs. Had to. They were so important to my staying in the cottage and staying sane that they absolutely must become the anchor of my new business in addition to remaining the anchor to my new life they already were.

Zack's singing was both off-key and perfect. For me, anyway. So my budding business became Off Key & Perfect. Let customers figure it out if they could. I knew the reason and that was all that mattered. Soon my website front page had a banner with music notes blazing across the top made up of all the things I'd imagined creating that I'd better get busy and actually make. And the rest of the website went smoothly due to my experience in marketing.

I soon filled out the government application to become an actual business with the name writ large and with a flourish. I sealed the envelope with another flourish and got it ready to mail to the state along with a check, of course, the next time I went to town. Then I leaned back and felt like I'd accomplished a major thing. And I had.

Summer was coming fast. The days were stretching longer each week and when I put that envelope in my purse to mail later I realized it was time for dinner. I actually cooked that day and ate on the deck and watched waves wash over the sandy beach and wipe it clean of whatever might have disturbed it before the last wave.

A hamburger was easy and it didn't matter that I had bread instead of a bun. A quick salad completed my dinner and I'd had enough pie during the day that I didn't need dessert. As I ate, watching the lake and the beach, I thought back on the day. And the pies. And the man I'd shared them with.

Off-key songs accompanied my meal and I listened and smiled and each song told me in stronger and still stronger terms that my nights of fear were over. Nothing could scare me now. The whisperer might come but he wouldn't scare me ever again.

When the sun finally dipped beneath the horizon, I cleaned up the dishes, closed the sliding glass doors to the deck and locked them tight, locked the front door and checked all the windows, making sure each and every dead bolt was thrown. It had nothing to do with the whisperer. It felt better that way. I took a shower because I'd been dumpster diving and it just seemed like a good thing to do. And I slid into bed and expected to sleep like a babe.

I did, too. Until the first whisper.

"Lexi."

I sat up, terrified even though I'd been so sure I'd never fear it again. But there was something about the sound of it. The evil of it. The pure evil.

"Lexi." The whisper was so sure of itself. So arrogant. So superior. And so frightening. "Lexi, dear. Are you there? Are you listening?" Followed by, "Of course you are, dear Lexi."

I pulled the blanket around me because it felt safer though I knew mere blankets wouldn't chase the whispers away. "Go away." I tried out my most authoritative voice. And failed because anyone listening would hear my fear.

"Oh Lexi," The whisperer laughed, a prolonged, evil sound. "You are so precious. I love it when you pretend to not be afraid." Another laugh, bouncing from wall to wall until my very being ached with fear. "You are afraid. So afraid."

"I'm not afraid of you."

Another laugh, this time louder, almost more than a whisper, followed by what turned to be one last comment. "I'm getting to you, aren't I, Lexi? You are afraid. You are more afraid each and every time I talk to you and that's as it should be."

"I'm not."

"You are and that's your weakness. Your fear. It'll wear you down, you know, until you are nothing but a shadow. And then you'll be mine, dear Lexi. Mine. Forever." Then it was gone and, like the other times, I knew somehow that it wouldn't return that night.

But I was terrified because some part of me knew it was right. I knew my fear would grow until it truly could somehow possess me. I wanted to puke. And, of course I couldn't sleep. Not after that.

I unlocked the sliding glass doors and stepped onto the deck. The night was dark. There was no moonlight reflecting on the lake, no silver touching the world in a reassuring way. So I turned on the outside light to give a feel of safety to the deck and I dragged a thick blanket outside and curled up with it on one of the lounges and just sat there and pretended everything would be alright even though it never would be alright again. Never.

Because if the whispers didn't stop even after the bravery Zack has instilled in me, then they never would and someday the whisperer would get what it wanted. Me. I didn't know how it would get me or what it would do with me once it had me but I knew it would happen and there was nothing I could do about it.

A sound broke the silent night. The sound of someone swimming. Whoever was out there in the night was swimming towards my beach. Because of the light? I considered turning it off but I needed its comfort so I left it on and hoped my visitor wouldn't be a murderer. Or worse.

The night dark swimmer reached shallow water and soon was walking through that shallow water to the beach. Then across it. Then across the small yard between the beach and the deck. Then Zack Slater climbed onto the deck and looked at me with a puzzled expression. "Why are you on your deck in the middle of the night wrapped in a blanket with a light on that must be attracting every insect in the area?"

"Why are you swimming in a really cold lake in the middle of the night without even a moon for light?" I got up and headed inside to get the largest towel I had because he was a really large man.

When I returned I handed it to him and he took it thankfully and wrapped himself in it. "I was taking a bath. Sort of. It's the only way to get clean until I get plumbing in the house."

I remembered the tent with that huge table in front of it. He must live there and tents don't have showers. Or much of any other of the amenities I enjoyed in my aunt's cottage.

But I had a whisperer in the cottage which was something he didn't have in his flimsy tent.

CHAPTER 7

"So?" He inspected me up, down and sidewise while toweling himself. "Are you going to tell me why you're on your deck in the middle of the night? I know you haven't been here all night because I'd have seen your light and I've been in the lake for the better part of an hour which means you just came out now." He waited and when I said nothing, he asked, "Are you going to tell me? Or is it a deep, dark secret?"

I could lie, of course, and say I'd decided to enjoy some time outside in the middle of the night with insects buzzing all around and driving me crazy. He'd know I was lying but would be too polite to argue. Or I could tell him the truth. I opened my mouth, not knowing what I'd say until the words came out. "Someone – or something – is keeping me awake."

He toweled himself dry enough to sit on the other lounge and lean close. "Who?" He didn't laugh and that made me feel good. Warm.

"I don't know who. Or what. It's more likely a 'what' than a 'who.' It's just a voice. Not a voice, even, just a whisper. But it comes every night and I can't sleep."

"You're having a recurring nightmare?"

"I thought so at first. But it's not. I know it's not."

"So some weirdo is making your life miserable. What does this weirdo say, exactly?"

"That it's going to take me."

"Huh?!"

"I know. It sounds insane. But it's happened every night since I came to the cottage. I thought it would end after today but it didn't."

"Why today?"

"Because it was such a good day. It was special. It's a truly evil whisper and I thought a good day would surely defeat evil. But it didn't, not this time, anyway. And I'm so sick and tired of it that I came out on the deck because it's better here, even with all the insects, than being inside listening to a whisper telling me it's going to do all kinds of terrible things."

"Some guy is threatening you." A statement, not a question.

"Not specifically. Just that I'm going to eventually belong to it but the things it says means I'm going to die. They must mean that." I watched him watching me. "I know it sounds ridiculous. But it's real. I swear it."

He thought for a long moment, towel wrapped around his shoulders and leaning close and staring at me as if that would tell him something. Probably whether I was insane or not.

Then he straightened back up abruptly. "I'll stay with you tonight. If you want."

I jumped at the offer. "I have a couch." I mentally measured the smallish couch in the cottage against his large frame. "Except it's too short for you. I'll sleep on the couch and give you the bed."

He shook his head. "I have a sleeping bag and an

air mattress in my tent. It'll only take a couple minutes to bring them over. And I'll bring Little Guy, if you are okay with him."

"Of course. Little Guy and I are great friends."

He disappeared around the forest between our places and soon returned with an armful of sleeping equipment in one arm and a very sleepy puppy in the other.

It only took minutes for him to spread his air mattress and sleeping bag on the floor of the main room of the cottage. I was glad I'd spent so much time finding places to store everything I'd brought with me when I arrived and what I'd found dumpster diving. Otherwise there'd have been no room.

He looked around. "Is this place bigger than it looks?"

"Why?"

"Where'd you put all your stuff? Your junk?"

I grinned. "Don't look in the closets. Or the corners. Or under anything at all."

"Okay. Everything is here somewhere. Hidden."

"Yep." I found myself drifting towards the coffee maker. "Want some coffee before we go to bed?"

"Of course." As if it was implicit that coffee was part of every social occasion. There had been a thermos on the table where he lived and worked. I'd have to remember that about Zack. He was a coffee addict.

"And donuts? I think I have some." His grin said donuts would be the perfect addition to coffee in the middle of the night. Turned out I didn't have donuts but did have chocolate cake from the same store as that first night when the whispers kept me up until dawn. I'd bought that cake's twin the next time I went to town and I brought it out now.

Zack's face lit up like a lightbulb when he saw the cake and his smile magnified that inner light that seemed to be a part of him. It was a thousand times brighter if such was possible.

There'd be no more whispers that night whether Zack was there or not. I knew it. The whisperer had never come more than once each night. And there weren't. Which was good because the tension in me unwound as the minutes and then an hour passed, during which we devoured the entire cake. I ate a quarter of it and Zack finished the other three quarters and I never mentioned that I'd eaten an entire cake the first night I was there.

But his presence was depressing in a way. His expression was easy to read and it said he didn't believe there'd truly been a whisperer. That I had a huge imagination but he liked me anyway. It stung that he thought I was a flighty female. Because I'm not.

But I reveled in the security of his large and capable body being so close when we turned off the lights and went to bed, he in his sleeping bag in the middle of the floor of the main room and me in the bedroom. With the door open because I felt safer that way. I'm normally not a coward. But after hearing the whispers that night after being so sure they'd never bother me again, I was afraid. Terrified. Perhaps the whisperer had already succeeded. Perhaps he'd already done what he needed to do. Perhaps I already belonged to him and acquiring the physical part of me was just a matter of time.

I slept late the next morning, my first truly restful night and it was due to Zack's presence. But the sun wouldn't let me sleep forever, even though the door was now closed, undoubtedly because Zack had decided to let me sleep. Through it I heard that lusty, off-kay voice singing what might have been a sea ballad. Or a dirge. Or something else entirely that I'd have loved to lie in bed and listen to forever except I'd have to get up to close the curtains against those bright rays and if I got up to do that I might as well stay up.

Not to mention the smell of frying bacon reminded me how hungry I was. When was the last time I'd eaten a decent breakfast? I couldn't remember. Not since arriving at the cottage. My stomach had been too queasy to eat decently, fault of the whispers. But not now.

So I showered quickly, pulled on jeans and a tee shirt, not bothering with shoes because I was inside, and dragged a brush through my hair until the tangles disappeared. I considered confining it with a bandanna but didn't because, after all, my hair is pretty when it's clean and free of knots and there was a good looking guy on the other side of that door. So I simply shook it loose and went to see what else was on the menu. Surely there'd be more than bacon.

"Will you make toast?" The casual question came at me as soon as I stepped into the main room. "I hope you like your eggs sunny side up because that's the only way I know how to make them."

"Yes to both toast and eggs." The bacon was on the side of the stove, keeping warm while eggs were frying. I breathed deeply of the morning and considered the main room that was now neat and tidy with Zack's bedding somewhere unseen and the table set for two. "There's juice somewhere in the refrigerator. I'll get it."

And glasses. Along with the toast, of course.

When the eggs were done he scooped them onto a platter with the bacon and turned to bring them to the table. And stopped. And stared. At me and I stopped, too, and our looks met for a moment before he continued on to the table and placed the platter in the exact center as I forced myself to move and bring the juice and toast while wondering what had just happened. What kind of man-woman thing had just filled the cottage with electricity and charged the sunny day with something special. And it had been special. No question about it.

Then the moment was gone and we were eating with gusto, me because I was starved and Zack because I suspected that was how he ate every single meal. The man was large and worked hard physically and needed every calorie that breakfast provided.

We talked. Not at first. We were too busy eating and pretending not to look at each other while surreptitiously examining everything about the person across the table. But eventually we slowed down and considered each other. And the cottage we were in.

Zack looked at the bathroom with absolute envy. "Must be nice." He sighed. "I don't have running water in my house yet. One of the problems with buying a fixer-upper."

"What else don't you have?"

"Electricity."

"How do you operate all those power tools I saw the other day?"

"I have a generator. It works for the hand tools and to charge batteries but that's about all."

I drank my orange juice and looked at him

speculatively over the rim of my glass. "How'd you like to take a shower? Now. Here. In my bathroom."

His eyes shone. "You mean it?" I nodded. "I'd love it." He tipped his head towards the lake gleaming in the over-the-top sunshine beyond the sliding glass doors. "The lake works but it's not the warmest." He shrugged. "It'll get warmer as summer comes but a nice, not shower would be absolute heaven."

He rose. "I'll get my stuff from my place. Be right back." He picked up his bedroll and headed towards the door.

"Wait." He turned to see what I wanted. "Leave it here." His brows knitted in a question. "For now. I have an idea. I'll run it past you when you return but you can leave your stuff here in the meantime."

He was puzzled but he dropped everything back to where it had been and trotted off to get a change of clothes and shaving stuff. When he returned he went straight to the bathroom and, just as I expected, was soon singing in the shower. I was glad he couldn't see how thoroughly turned on I was by that ridiculous semblance of music.

When he was done, leaving the bathroom neat and tidy, he stood over me where I sat. "What did you want to talk about?"

I looked up at him. Way up. I took a deep breath and went for it. "I know you don't believe I heard whispers last night. Or any night." Another deep breath because it was hard to talk about it. "But I did hear them. And they will come back, I know they will. And I don't want to be alone when they do."

He didn't say anything. Didn't agree with me or disagree. Just waited with his arms crossed for the rest of what I had to say. "So I'm wondering if you'd like to stay here at night. I'm hoping you will. I'm not usually a coward but I am now and another person in the cottage will be appreciated. And you can use the bathroom and we can cook regular meals in the kitchen and you'll have a warm place to sleep."

He grinned. "My tent is comfortable but this cottage is better and a bathroom and kitchen would be absolute luxury." The grin grew until it reached his eyes. "So my answer is 'yes' and I'll bring the rest of my stuff later today and I can't thank you enough because I suspect I'm getting the better part of the deal."

"No you aren't. I am." My voice was low. Perhaps he didn't hear. Or perhaps he was just being polite by not saying what he thought of my rabid imagination.

"So that's settled. I'll help with the dishes." And the two of us cleaned up side by side in a companionable silence and then he headed for his house to get it one step closer to being built while I unearthed some of the things I'd hidden previously. It was time to lay them out and figure out what useful or beautiful things I could turn them into.

CHAPTER 8

The single use plastic bags I'd been saving for the better part of the year would become fashionable totes once I turned them into plastic yarn. Thanks, Grandma, for teaching me how to crochet. The bottles and boxes and other plastic things I'd managed to clean up enough to not be a health hazard would be melted into coasters once I added a little color and or glitter before they hardened.

I wasn't sure what to do with the old leather jackets I'd picked up at a yard sale but was sure I could make something out of them. Stuffed bears? Purses? I'd figure it out. And of course, the old broken lamps could be rewired, repaired and refitted with new handmade shades that would become my signature items and would make awesome additions to any room.

I picked my way through my prized collection of junk that littered the entire floor now that I'd brought it all out to examine it. It would have to be removed before Zack could sleep there that night, of course, because there wasn't enough space left for his sleeping bag, but just looking at it all made me feel better and better about my decision to go into business for myself.

When the middle of the day rolled around I decided

to check on Zack and ask what he wanted for lunch. After all, I'd said we'd cook regular meals in my kitchen and I wanted him to know that meant three meals a day and that I was good with doing the cooking. Though if he wanted to continue making breakfast it would be alright with me. I never was a morning person.

I'd heard his singing all morning and I'd spent as much time picturing him working on his fixer-upper as I had deciding what to do with my carefully collected junk.

As I rounded the thicket between our places I saw him, shirtless, filling in the holes where he'd removed rotten walls with new two-by-fours. The old house was already looking better than any time I remembered and it was still in the bare bones stage of building.

He somehow knew I was there and turned. "Need something?" I shook my head and explained about lunch. His eyes widened. "I get lunch, too?" I nodded. "I'll be there as soon as I get these nailed in place."

I returned to the cottage with warmth pooling in my middle, both from the way the man I'd just left made me feel and from the sense of security he projected. As if he could defeat evil without getting winded. Which he probably could.

When he stepped into the cottage, he stopped. Stared at all that junk. And shook his head. "I knew you had a lot of stuff but this – this is scary much."

"It's a start."

He bent enough to examine everything minutely, as if each and every thing was important. A treasure. "I'm sure it'll all be lovely." Then he added, unable to hide the tone of doubt in his voice, "Eventually. Probably."

Then he shook his head again. "Though I admit I can't picture what most of it will become."

That led to me explaining my ideas. I watched his face because he was the first person I'd let into my dreams and I wanted to know if my ideas were too ridiculous. But each time I pointed out what I planned to do with something he would nod seriously and say it sounded like a good idea.

When I was finished, he asked, "Why do you only have small things? Don't you want to make anything larger? Like furniture? You mentioned furniture."

I explained how figuring out shipping costs and packing boxes meant I wasn't ready to tackle furniture yet. He agreed, then said, "A guy in town mentioned a flea market every weekend. Evidently you can sell anything there. Even refurbished furniture and I'm sure yours would be gorgeous and would sell like hot cakes. Because everything you make will be beautiful and sell for a fortune."

I almost laughed. He was being so nice. He didn't have a clue what quality my work would be but he praised it anyway. But I pointed out the problem with his suggestion. "Furniture is heavy."

He spread his legs apart and folded his arms as he looked me up and down. "I can carry it." He shrugged. "If you want to sell it at the flea market."

I said I'd think about it but knew I'd not do it. He'd be great for a while but what would I do when we parted ways? And we would part ways because people always do.

He stepped carefully among my treasures, heading for the table and lunch. "Want me to bring anything for supper? I have canned just about everything due to the fact I have no electricity so have no refrigerator or freezer."

"Why don't you bring whatever you have? Anything will do."

Lunch was comfortable and lasted longer than necessary because we somehow found so many things to talk about that we were surprised when we noted the time. But we managed to get some work done that afternoon and when he returned for dinner we had meat from my refrigerator and beans from one of his cans and it was a great meal, finished off with cookies from town though I made a mental note to make some myself as soon as I could find the time, even though I'm not usually big on housewifely chores.

But baking cookies suddenly appealed to me. Because he was so large. It would surely take a lot of food to fill him up and cookies qualified. No other reason to spend time baking. Definitely not any nesting impulse on my part.

It was dark when we went to bed, which meant it was pretty late because long summer evenings had arrived and sunlight stretched far into the night. But as I pulled the blankets around me I was relaxed. And I wasn't afraid. Because as the dark grew darker and the stars came out in the velvet, moonless sky I promised myself I'd get some sleep. Because hopefully there'd be no whispers. Surely the whisperer would know Zack was there and would stay away.

I was wrong. The first whisper said my name, soft and evil. "Lexi."

I rolled over, my stomach clenching. I was glad the door to the main room was open, with Zack's black form visible in the middle of the floor. I thought he moved but wasn't sure. I hoped so. I hoped he was awake. And listening.

The whisper continued. "Lexi. Dear, dear Lexi." I sat up. "Did you miss me, Lexi? Did you miss our little conversations?" Followed by laughter, low and gross and evil.

I stared unseeingly into the black night and spoke with what I hoped was bravery but was probably only loud. "I'm not afraid of you. Not now. Not ever."

Did Zack hear? Was he awake? Yes, he was. He rolled soundlessly towards me, rising slightly from his bedding on the floor and propping himself on an elbow. Listening.

"You're so brave, Lexi. So very brave, little girl." Laughter echoed from wall to wall. "Nice try but it won't work, you silly girl. You stupid child. Because nothing will help. Not your brave words, not having a friend stay with you no matter how large he is or how brave. Nothing ever helped my other victims and nothing will help you now." So the whisperer knew Zack was there. "Nothing can save you from me." More laughter, even more evil. "You will be mine, Lexi. Mine forever. I will take your beautiful self, inhale your essence and give your soul to Satan so you will spend eternity in Hell."

"You'll never get me." My words had steel but only because I wasn't alone. Because Zack was there.

"Oh, Lexi. Sweet Lexi. I will get you. Of course I will. I never fail." Then, as other nights, the whispers ended with, "Lexiiii. Lexiiii." Then there was silence and, the same as those other nights, I knew somehow that the whisperer had gone back to wherever he'd come from.

I sat up in my bed and rocked back and forth in an attempt to comfort myself but, without hearing him get up, I felt Zack beside me. He pulled me close. He hugged me. Stilled me. Shushed me.

His voice was low. "You were right. There is a weirdo after you." I let myself melt against his body. He was a rock. A bulwark. "But don't worry, Lexi. He won't get you. Not now. Not ever."

He was faceless in the night but he was there and that was the important thing. I clung to him. "What can I do? It's just a voice. A whisper. Nothing substantial. But what if he's right? What if he can get to me? I know he doesn't exist, not really, but what can I do against something that doesn't exist?"

"I don't know. Not yet. But I promise you this particular weirdo isn't going to do whatever his sick mind has planned. Not now. Not ever. Not while I'm around."

I relaxed against him and somehow, perhaps a long time later or possibly in just a few minutes, I never knew which, I fell asleep and when I awoke the sun was bright and the world was fresh and safe and Zack was sound asleep on his bed in the middle of my cottage floor, his slight snore saying the world was normal and good.

I stepped around his sleeping body, determined to start breakfast. He'd made me feel safe during the night. The least I could do was make breakfast. But it didn't happen.

He snorted and woke up. Sat up. Stretched and looked around, instantly aware of where he was and what had happened during the night. He leaned his elbows on his knees and looked up at me as I tried to reach the refrigerator through the maze that was now my cottage main room so I could pull out bacon and eggs and whatever else looked edible.

"Forget cooking." There was no sleep in his voice. None at all. He'd gone from full sleep to full wakefulness in seconds. "You were right about the whispers and I apologize for doubting you." He examined me in my shocking pink nightgown and tried not to grin. Failed completely. Looked around the room and let his grin grow and pretended my dumpster treasures were behind that smile instead of my ridiculous nightwear. "What say we head to town for breakfast? My treat."

"It would be easier than trying to cook in this disaster of a room."

"We can take turns in the bathroom and then head out." His face said time spent in a real bathroom with hot running water would be a luxury. I should have given him the first turn but I was closer to the bathroom so I ducked in and got ready for the day. But I spent as little time there as possible and made sure to leave him plenty of hot water. After all, that large body of his probably required a lot more hot water than mine.

In less time than I'd expected, we were on our way to town in Zack's old but rugged pickup, my hand slightly out the window to catch the warm wind and the sun's rays. He noticed. "My momma always said a woman needs sunshine and treats when she's feeling down and I happen to know the café on the beach has awesome sticky buns."

"And how do you know this interesting fact?"

"Because I love good sticky buns and can zero in on them from miles away." His grin stretched across his face and soon we were at one of the outside tables at that café with chocolate milk and sticky buns that meant we had to lick our fingers clean. No forks, of course, because they would be an insult to such an amazing breakfast.

Across the table, Zack smiled and smiled and smiled and I wondered and hoped that his expression was at least partly because of me and not entirely because we were eating beside the beach and watching the waves sweep it clean each time they washed ashore.

Town hadn't awakened yet. Too early in the morning and not yet tourist season. During the summer it would be humming even this early but the cottages along the lake were mostly empty and the resorts were still being readied for the season. So we had the café and the beach to ourselves.

Until a man with dark hair meandered along the beach, throwing stones into the lake and dodging the waves as he neared us. He stopped. Looked at us. Decided we were worth talking to. And approached.

"Hi." He looked us up and down. Now that he was close, I saw that his dark hair had streaks of gray. He was older than I'd thought. "Visiting?"

Zack shook his head and licked the last of the frosting from his fingers. He sighed in ecstasy. "Nope. We live a ways up the beach." He tipped his head towards our respective houses.

"The old Adams place?"

Zack nodded. "I believe that's who owned it before me."

"Been empty a long time." The stranger dropped into a third chair and examined us. Then he examined just me. "You?"

"I'm staying in my aunt's cottage next door to Zack." He nodded but said nothing.

"She's starting a business." Zack offered the information as one would a precious gem and the stranger gave me more than a cursory look as Zack finished with, "Refurbishing old things."

"Junk," I added to be explicit and the stranger nodded as if that made all the sense in the world and that polite nod decided me that I liked him. I smiled brightly to encourage friendship.

CHAPTER 9

After the stranger left, Zack asked what I thought about him. I shivered. "He seemed nice but the whisperer is male so I'm leery of any and all men now." I gave him a look of apology. "Except you, of course. I know you."

He smiled and rubbed the back of his neck. "I agree and for the same reason. He seems nice enough. But someone is harassing you. This guy could have been out for a walk and decided to be friendly. Or he could have been inspecting his intended victim."

There was nothing to say after that and the silence dragged on for a long time as we watched the waves on the beach across the street from the café and I finished my sticky bun. Then I decided to end the awkward silence. "I thank you for staying with me at night and also for helping me collect junk. I know what helping me will cost you considering how busy you are with your house."

"It's true I need to get it closed to the weather."

"How long will that take? Is time likely to be a problem? Perhaps you shouldn't help me. A house is more important."

"Should be closed in soon. I've got all the

materials. A week or so. By the time summer turns hot." He looked at me briefly, then back at the lake. "It's not a problem. I can help you."

He stared at the horizon instead of at me. "When my house is tight to the weather I'll be able to camp inside and not worry about rain or wind or other weather problems. Surely by then this idiot who's bothering you will be unmasked and you'll be able to say goodbye to me and I won't have to sleep in a tent."

I thought about that tent. "You're sleeping inside now. A cottage instead of a house. But I wonder. Do you miss the stars at night? And moonlight on the water?" Which he must see if he slept outside instead of in his tent and somehow I thought he did because he came across as an outdoors kind of guy. I could picture him lying on the ground and staring at the night sky.

He turned towards me. His eyes were the bright blue of the lake under the summer sun. "Yes, I'll miss those things, though not the sand in my sleeping bag or the dampness when the fog comes in. Or the frogs that crawl over me on their way to wherever they're going."

He examined our empty plates and gave his fingers one last lick. Our eyes met and we silently agreed that sticky buns are one of life's luxuries. "I suppose we should go home and get busy."

He dropped me off at the cottage and then continued on to his house. But instead of hearing singing and hammers, I soon saw him rounding the trees between our places as he came to where I stood on the deck fashioning a workspace. Trying to fashion one. It wasn't going well. The deck was small compared to what I needed it to hold.

He examined the deck with something like awe. "I

meant to ask earlier, before we were interrupted by that guy during breakfast." He continued, undecided whether to scowl because he was uncertain about our morning visitor or smile because it was a nice day. "The first thing I did when I started working on the house, even before doing anything on the house itself, was to add to the garage. It's three times as large now as originally and the extra space is a fairly large workshop."

"Every guy needs a workshop." Like my father and brothers. "And it must help with remodeling the house."

He nodded briefly. "Mostly it's for my new business. The one I'm going to start once the house is livable."

"The handyman business." I decided to be honest. "I didn't know that was an actual business."

"Of course it is and with all the cottages along the lakeshore with owners who don't want to spend their vacations fixing things that broke during the winter I suspect there'll be lots of work for me." He took a deep breath. "Anyway, the reason I came here now is to offer part of the workshop to you since I've got space and you need some. I'd have said something earlier except I was distracted by our visitor in town. They guy who probably isn't the idiot bothering you but since he's a human male and whoever is scaring you is a man I spent the entire time trying to read him." He raked his hair. "I think he's a nice guy."

Then he looked at the jumble of things spread out on the deck after which he peered through the sliding glass doors to the main room of the cottage that was also full of junk. "I suspect you can use a little extra space and the workshop comes with a workbench and outlets for hand tools and everything."

"It sounds like paradise."

"I thought you'd feel that way and it's usable now, just with a generator instead of working electric outlets on the walls." He tipped his head to one side. "So what about it? Are you interested?"

"I'll start moving my stuff immediately."

"I can help."

"You don't have to do that." Guilt bled through me. "You have a house to finish. How did you put it? You need to get it 'tight to the weather.'"

"It won't take long to move your stuff."

I considered the junk we stood among. "Yes it will."

He reddened.. "Okay, you have a lot of stuff. But if we use my pickup we can do it in one trip." He silently counted everything. "Or two. Or three."

He smiled then and, as always, his smile lit up the day. "The sooner we get started the sooner you can make something amazing out of all -- *this*." He rubbed the back of his neck again, a gesture I was now sure was a nervous habit when he was uncertain. Or embarrassed. "It'll be interesting to see what you come up with." He turned redder and, as the other times, I had no idea what was behind it. I hoped it was me but pushed that thought away. "Amazing treasures, I'm sure."

Moving everything from my cottage to his workshop required two trips and the bed of the pickup was piled high each time. How'd I manage to accumulate so much stuff in such a short time? "My car couldn't possibly hold this much stuff when I came here."

As Zack piled the last of my junk in a corner of his workshop he said, diplomatically, "We got a lot when we went dumpster diving the other day." Then he brightened, casting a look around the empty space still left in his brand new workshop. "There's room for furniture if you want to refurbish some."

All that space was tempting and he'd made the move easy, doing most of the work while I enjoyed watching his muscles move under his inevitable tee shirt. "Maybe." Being in his workshop would increase the odds of him continuing to help. So maybe furniture would be a practical addition to my business. "I'll check the dumpsters the next time we go to town."

"What about today? Now?"

"You haven't done a thing to your house today. I don't want to make you wait any longer than necessary. Or have frogs crawl over you."

"I'm sleeping in your cottage. Remember? No frogs. Besides, I can take a day off if I so choose and I'm kind of invested in your business now, or I will be if you refinish furniture because I promised to do the heavy lifting. So I'd like to see what the future holds for our partnership."

Partnership. The word had a nice ring to it and the more I thought about it the more I realized there was no reason we couldn't work together for a long time, especially if I decided to stay in the area year around.

I'd have to find a place to live because the cottage wasn't winterized but I was fairly sure it wouldn't be a problem once the tourists left and the town shut down for the season. Surely someone would have a room to rent.

We had lunch in the cottage, making sandwiches

side by side and enjoying the fact that it was now free of junk. Then we climbed into his pickup and headed back to town. We took his truck because we just might find some furniture to bring back.

I thought that was optimistic but it turned out to be the day for trash collecting and at one house we found a table that was being tossed. We asked the owners if they were okay with us taking it and they were fine with it, mentioning how one person's trash was another's treasure.

And the café where we'd had sticky buns was tossing out their damaged chairs. After examining them, Zack thought he could make them good as new and my brain went into overdrive with ideas for turning them into artsy accent pieces for someone's cottage.

We celebrated by buying pop at the café and taking it to the town beach where we sat on the sand and looked along the shoreline towards our respective houses. We didn't live far from town. Not really. We should be able to see them. Or so we figured. But for some reason, we couldn't though we could identify cottages near our places.

"It's as if there's something in the air. Just where our houses are located. Heat waves, maybe?"

"There aren't heat waves anywhere else."

"But the air is opaque between our houses and here."

We squinted. We stared. We shaded our eyes with our hands. But nothing could make our homes come clear, or the tiny forest between them that should have been easy to find because it was much larger than any building.

"That's odd." We turned at the voice and saw the

stranger of the morning looking where we were looking. "It's like something is in the air." He pointed to the shimmer that hid our homes. "A curtain. Water falling. Something quite strange."

I jumped. "I didn't see you."

"I saw you two and was curious why you came back to town." He hunkered down beside us as if we were old friends. "By the way, my name's Dennis Penning and I grew up in Lewistown, though I spent a fair amount of my working life elsewhere."

After we introduced ourselves, he asked, "Are those your cottages that you're trying so hard to see from here and failing totally because of whatever is out there hanging in midair?"

I said they were. "I'm staying in my aunt's cottage and Zack's house is next door."

Dennis Penning settled on the beach and stared. Squinted as we'd done. And finally shook his head as a puzzled frown creased his forehead. "It's odd." He stared some more. "I'm sure I've seen this phenomenon before but I can't remember where or what caused it. Except --"

He went silent. After a moment, I prodded him. "Except what? Do you know something about whatever is preventing us from seeing clearly?"

Dennis Penning pressed his lips together. He didn't want to say what he was about to tell us. "Except, as I remember it, whatever it is, is bad. It was when I was in Africa, I believe. My wife and I were missionaries."

"You've seen it before?" The hair on the back of my neck stood up as Zack considered the speaker. First a whisperer in the night. Now a shimmer. "You say it's bad. In what way?"

Dennis shrugged. "I can't remember other than that it's not good. Like a bad omen or something similar. Some tribal kind of thing, maybe?" He rose and dusted sand from himself. "And that's all and surely it's just a coincidence. Sorry if I'm spoiling the day for you but that weird haze is disconcerting." He backed a few steps. "I think I'll be on my way before I remember just what about it was so awful. Though I'm sure this is different. Just a haze. Nothing important." He smiled but without humor. "Forget what I said and have a good day."

Then he was gone, leaving Zack and me looking at each other and then, again, at the shimmer that created a translucent curtain between the beach and our homes. Bright and transparent but with a dark backlit effect. Like Dennis had said, it was weird. And it only covered our houses. Just ours. As I looked closer, I changed that to just my cottage. Zack's house seemed to also be behind the odd shimmer because it was nearby. But when I examined it closely, I realized the shimmer was meant for my place. Just mine. I almost lost my lunch.

CHAPTER 10

We gave up trying to see our houses from town and I declared we had enough furniture to get a good start on our partnership. So we took everything back to Zack's workshop. He checked the chairs and said it would be relatively easy to fix them. "Large screws and really good glue when I put them together again."

"Let me refinish them while they are in pieces. It'll be easier." He nodded that he understood and started to take them apart. "No." I put out a hand to stop him.

"No?"

"You have a house to finish. I have enough small stuff to keep me busy for the rest of the summer without the furniture so there's no hurry to get it done."

"The first flea market is in two weeks. We should have something then."

"Do at least some work on your house first so I don't feel guilty." I folded my arms in front of me and stared at him. Glared. Narrowed my eyes and dared him to argue.

He grinned broadly. "Okay, boss lady."

He gave me a lazy salute and disappeared in the direction of a pile of two by fours that would soon be nailed across the open spaces in the walls and when sheets of plywood were nailed to them the house would be almost closed in against the weather. A lovely, carved door had mysteriously appeared. Windows would complete the job.

The house was changing fast. I could see progress as the hours passed while I puttered with my small items. Zack could work on the chairs soon but the house would also get done. The summer was shaping up nicely.

With going to town twice, hanging out on the beach for a while, moving my stuff to Zack's workshop and then getting started on my business, the day passed quickly. The long summer day meant we could work late into the evening. We had a quick meal of leftovers heated in the microwave. Then we went to bed. And to sleep. I was tired. I needed a good night's sleep.

I slept for a few hours. Until the whispers started.

"Lexi."

I sat up, comforted by the fact that Zack was awake and listening but mostly by the fact that he was near. That I wasn't dealing with whatever was threatening me alone.

"Dear, dear Lexi. You've been foolish." A whispered sigh, then, "What am I going to do with such a foolish girl?"

Zack was beside me without me hearing him come. He spoke quietly. "He's playing mind games. Putting you down. Trying to make you think you are worthless." His breath was warm as he pushed my hair aside so I could hear his murmured words. "Don't let him succeed."

So I laughed as loud as possible considering I was terrified and it was the middle of the night. "I am not foolish. Not at all. Guess you don't know me."

Beside me, Zack nodded approval. "That's it, Lexi. Keep it up. Let him know you aren't afraid."

The whisperer heard Zack. "Your friend can't help you, Lexi. No one can." Another laugh was drawn out in the dark. "Because you are mine, Lexi. Mine."

Before I could reply, it continued. "I'll wait a while, though. Until you are weaker. It's easier that way. Less resistance. And you will resist though it won't make any difference in the end. My chosen ones always do. But you will be mine no matter what you do and there's nothing you or your friend can do about it. You will be mine forever."

Zack straightened. Stared into the dark room, anger vibrating from his every pore as he spoke loudly and with scorn. "Whoever you are – *whatever* you are – hear this. Lexi will never belong to you. Never. You might as well accept that and leave. Now. Because you can't have her. Not while I'm around."

I heard what happened next. Felt it. Saw it. The air in the room was sucked out in one huge whoosh. For a moment we were suspended in a vacuum and unable to breathe. Then the air returned like a hurricane that almost knocked us over as that whispery laugh returned with full force.

I knew what had happened. For a moment it had been surprised. Stunned. Zack had gotten to it. So we knew what it said next was part bluster. We could hear the lessening of certainty though its words were as boastful as ever as it whispered to Zack. "I'm more than enough for you, little man."

Its next words were more self-assured but there was still a tinge of worry. "Remember earlier today?

When you two sat on the beach and looked for Lexi's house? You couldn't see it because I hid it behind a veil."

I gasped and bent over as if I'd been sucker punched. "You did that? You can make the air shimmer?"

The whisper that followed was self-assured, the whisperer having regained its boastfulness and I knew the shock in my voice had done that. Had given it back its full power. "I did indeed, little Lexi, as a small demonstration of my power. Very small. But make no mistake, Lexi, that was only one thing. I can do more. Much more. I can do whatever I choose. I can have whoever I choose and I choose you, Lexi." It repeated its words. "I choose you."

Zack's arms were around me, holding me so tight I could barely breathe as his breath close to my ear deliberate and slow, vibrated with anger. He shouted into the dark. "You're one sick bastard, whoever you are. One sick, sexual pervert. A real psycho." And then he murmured to me, "Don't worry, Lexi. He'll not get you. I won't let him."

The whisperer laughed, a twisted, evil sound that echoed from wall to wall. "Not sexual at all. I outgrew that years ago. Centuries ago. Eons ago. No indeed, I want something entirely different from Lexi. Something much more basic."

"What, you bastard?" Zack's shout was louder. Angrier. His arms around me were tighter. His body tense and fierce. "What do you want from Lexi?"

The silence that followed was brutal. The blackness grew blacker, the faint light from the few stars outside disappeared and the world became a well of darkness so complete there was no up or down or anything except Zack and me clinging to one another because without that we'd disappear in that nothingness.

Then the whisperer spoke again. "I want Lexi's essence to feast upon. To give me sustenance. Then I want her soul. Her beautiful, lovely soul. It will be my gift to Satan."

"You can't have it. None of it."

"There's where you're wrong. I need her essence and Satan wants her soul." We felt rather than heard the whisperer considering whether to say more. Then it did. "Her essence will feed me. I need it. The beauty of that part of her. The vibrancy of it. It will nourish me. Keep me alive. You see, without sustenance every so often I will die."

"Take me, you bastard." Zack rose from the bed, still holding me as he dared the darkness to continue and, oddly, as he spoke, the black grew a little bit less, not quite so deep, not so complete. "If you can."

"No," the whisperer said in what would have been a sad voice if it wasn't so evil. "Lexi is sweet. Innocent. Unlike you, she is trusting." There was a pause. "Her trust makes her vulnerable. Easy prey." Another pause was followed by, "And make no mistake about it, she is prey. Her essence will be mine and she will die but I will live because of her and Hell will be her home forever."

And then the whisperer disappeared. The blackness returned to the normal dark of night with faint starlight seen through the square of the window and the outlines of furniture visible here and there. And Zack and I simply sat on the bed, stunned and silent because what was there to say after what we'd been told?

"He blocked the houses from our view," Zack said slowly, finally. "He did it." The question of how such a thing could be accomplished was in his voice if not his words.

I thought back to our time at the beach. "Dennis Penning was familiar with the shimmer. He knew it was bad." I turned into Zack. "How did he know?"

"I don't know but we're going to find out just as soon as we can get back to town. Tomorrow." He glanced at the clock on the wall. "Today, actually." It was past midnight.

"I won't sleep any more tonight."

"Yes you will. I'll stay. You'll be safe."

I moved to one side of the bed to make room for him. "Thank you."

He dropped onto the blankets and pulled them over me while remaining on top of them himself. Then he relaxed. I knew he was intentionally putting me at ease so I'd sleep. I also knew – because each day I knew him more and more – that he'd not sleep himself. Instead he'd keep watch for the rest of the night.

He'd give up his own sleep to make me feel safe. I didn't want him to do that. I should make it clear that he needed his rest as much as I needed mine. But I didn't. I wasn't that brave. I said nothing. Instead I let him lie on the blankets wide awake so I could sleep even though I knew I'd not sleep any more that night because how could I when I'd just been told that not only my body but my very soul was about to be forfeit?

Except I did sleep. Because of Zack. Because he would do whatever was needed to keep me safe and that was worth more than I could possibly imagine or ever repay. So in spite of my fears I fell into peaceful, dreamless slumber and only woke when the sun streaming through the window in the morning told me it was time to get up.

The other side of the bed was empty, Zack was gone and I heard that lovely, wonderful off-key singing in the kitchen while smelling bacon frying. I smiled and wondered how I'd gotten so lucky as to have for a neighbor an amazing and totally untalented musician who could also cook.

We dawdled over breakfast. We were in no hurry to clean up afterwards. We found ourselves reluctant to continue our work where we'd left it the day before.

It was a long time before we faced the fact that what we'd learned from the whisperer the night before had been so mind blowing that the world we woke up to wasn't the same one we went to bed in the night before.

It was Zack who finally put the last clean dish in the cupboard, wiped the table for the dozenth time, turned to me, and said, "It'll be okay, Lexi. You'll be fine. Ignore what that idiot said last night."

I dropped into a chair and picked up the crocheting I'd been working on whenever I had a few extra minutes. The tote I was making from used plastic bags that should sell like hot cakes because they were both useful and lovely. But I just stared at it as if trying to remember what it was and why I was working on it. "I suppose so."

He came beside me and stooped until our eyes were level. "I promise you that he won't succeed in his stupid, cockamamy scheme." He scowled. "He wants to steal your soul?" Lines appeared between his eyes. "Really? How lame is that."

"It happens. I've heard of it happening."

"It's your soul, yours, and it's not for sale, nor is it lying around for thieves to steal."

"Do you know that for sure?"

The crease between his eyes grew deeper and he used the pure force of his personality to make me look at him. "I know because I'll make it be the truth even if it isn't yet." His eyes narrowed. "I promise you, Lexi Tremaine, that no idiot vampire or demon or whatever he is will ever take any part of you. Not a single hair on your head. Not a smile. Not a breath of the air you breathe. Because if it tries anything at all, it'll have to deal with me and I'm very good at defeating any and all adversaries." He paused a moment. "Just ask the guys I served with. They'll tell you. I'm good, Lexi. Very good."

I couldn't look away, not if I tried and I had no reason to try. "Okay."

He relaxed and the world I knew returned and I realized the lake outside was just as it had been the day before and the waves were just as white and the beach just as clean. Nothing had changed overnight. Not really. And I knew this would continue to be true because Zack had just made a promise and I trusted him.

He smiled and rose and said, "I suppose we should get something done today." But neither of us made a move. Even though we'd got past it, the encounter during the night had sapped us both of the energy to do anything.

CHAPTER 11

I looked past Zack to the room that was no longer cluttered with junk. My eyes fell on my computer in the alcove that was now my office that I'd told Zack he could also use if he needed an internet connection. He'd said he wasn't at that stage yet but maybe after he got his house to a point where he could neglect it enough to get started on his handyman business he might take me up on my offer.

I said, "I'm going to do some research."

He followed my look to the computer. "What will you look up? Demons? Devils? Djinns? Ignorant idiots who get their kicks frightening pretty women?"

Zack thought I was pretty? I smiled inside. "I don't know. All of those things."

"I'll help."

"You have a house to get closed to the weather."

"I have a neighbor who's being threatened." He didn't repeat that I was pretty, but he'd said it once so my inner smile remained. Now he stretched and sighed. "But I'm kind of tired. Not a lot of sleep last night. I shouldn't be climbing ladders and doing stuff that could land me in a hospital should I fall asleep on the job."

He hadn't slept because of me. A river of guilt

poured through me. "You should take a nap." I managed a smile. It took effort but I did it without it slipping because I wanted him to know I was okay so he could take some time for himself. That he could rest. That he deserved a break. "By the time you wake up I might have found out some stuff."

"We should look for that guy in town. Dennis Penning. Find out what he knows. If anything." He looked longingly towards the bedroom. "But I could use a couple hours sleep. So if you're sure – "

"I owe you a nap." He didn't argue.

I put down my crocheting and waited pointedly for him to head for the bedroom and when he realized I wasn't going to move until he did, he went there and dropped onto the bed and promptly fell asleep.

I had to find a spare blanket to cover him with because he'd not even crawled between the sheets. He'd been that tired. Once the blanket was over him I stayed for a long time just watching him sleep. I didn't know why doing so made me feel better but it did.

While he slept I learned a lot about demons, devils, djinns and other unworldly evil beings. Most of the sites were filled with nonsense but there was enough good information that by the time he woke I knew the authorities agreed with what the whisperer had said. "They suck people's essence and devour them for food and what's left – their souls -- ends up in Hell."

"That's what Nutso told you last night. That it wanted your soul so it could live. Guess he was being honest." He added, "I'd never have believed such beings existed if I hadn't talked with one myself."

"They look for vulnerable people. All the articles said so." I wrapped my arms around myself and rocked back and forth. I didn't want to think of myself as vulnerable. But evidently I was.

"They look for easy prey and evidently you fit the profile." He gave me an expectant look. "In what way, exactly, did the internet say you are perfect for soul sucking?"

"There are several thoughts on the subject."

Zack looked over the printouts and pointed to a few key words. "Innocence is a big one."

"I'm not a child."

"There are degrees of innocence. Compared to me you are an innocent." He read more. "And trusting. It says here it's easier to steal a trusting person's soul than someone like me who's seen enough bloodshed that any trust I might have had was long ago ground out of me."

"That's sad."

He was surprised at my comment. "It's realistic."

"And sad." We went silent for a moment, each with our own thoughts. Then I continued. "I choose to trust people. I trust you. If I didn't then I'd be in a lot worse situation than I'm in. I'd be alone."

"That's true. So sometimes trust is good." He rocked back on his heels. "I promise that you can trust me. You should trust me. You just shouldn't trust anyone else."

"Trust isn't something I can turn on and off on command."

"Which is why he targeted you. Because you can't turn it off." He moved uncomfortably. "You can try. You should try. Maybe it'll work."

"I can't change who I am. What I am."

He sighed and rubbed the back of his neck. "Okay. It was just an idea." He dropped his hand to his side.

"I'm glad you are who you are. What you are. I like the person in front of me. It would just be better for you if you weren't such prime pickings for a demon. Devil. Djinn. Whatever is whispering in the night and wants your soul."

He looked at the clock. "If we head out now, we can have lunch at that café in town. Maybe someone there knows Dennis Penning. He said he's local. There's still time to track him down and find out what he knows that might help us."

I liked his choice of words. *Us.* As if we were in this thing together, which, when I thought on it, we were because that was how he'd been describing us from the beginning. Zack Slater said *us* and when Zack said something was so, that pretty much meant it was a fact because though I didn't know much about him – yet – I knew he spoke truth. Totally. Which meant we were a team. A pair. A couple. And unbeatable. It was a good feeling.

At the café we had biscuits and gravy and strawberry shortcake for dessert. Zack's idea. What was wrong with dessert after breakfast? Nothing. "Local strawberries," the server informed us. At our expressions of disbelief because it was still too early for berries of any kind, she explained. "From the greenhouse at the edge of town."

We each had two servings of shortcake heaped with strawberries. Zack ate both of his with gusto and finished my second when I couldn't. "Got to keep the local economy healthy and if eating strawberries will help then I'm in." He patted his flat stomach. "Besides, I love strawberries."

"Will you grow them when your house is

finished?”

“I might. Thanks for the idea. I’ll even share if you provide the shortcakes.”

How had we gone from terror during the night to strawberries at one of the outdoor tables near the town beach? Tight muscles relaxed as we lingered over empty plates and still more coffee and wondered without saying so how to find Dennis Penning.

I was about to suggest we ask the café owners if they knew him when, lo and behold, he meandered along the main street in town until he ended up at our table. And recognized us. And stopped. And dropped into an empty chair. “Hi, guys. You have good taste in food. This café is amazing.”

“It’s also the only one open this early in the season.”

“That too.” Dennis leaned back and clasped his hands behind his head. “And how have you been since I saw you last?” As if we were the best of friends. Which perhaps we were. It was a small town, after all, and the knowledge that we were local instead of summer people might have given us instant access to some exalted status in the local social hierarchy.

“It’s interesting that you asked,” Zack said in the kind of voice that said there was more. “And even more interesting that you knew about the shimmer over the lake that prevented us from seeing our houses.”

Dennis sat up straight. His smile disappeared. A tension went through his body. Because he remembered the shimmer. But all he said was, “Tell me.”

So Zack did, from the night he’d been swimming and came to see why my yard light was on to what had happened last night and what research had revealed.

Dennis listened without saying anything. When he was done, Zack gave our new acquaintance a measured look. "So what do you think? Are we insane?"

"Not at all." Not the answer we'd hoped for.

We three sat quietly for a long time, looking over the lake and the town nestled along the shore. Then Dennis Penning gave a great sigh and said, "I'd kind of hoped that I wouldn't have to deal with this stuff any more."

"You've dealt with it before?"

"Somewhat. Not specifically but I knew people who did when I was a missionary. Native people have superstitions and everyone knows evil when they see it."

"Do you know what we can do?"

Dennis bit his lower lip. "Not specifically. Not at the moment. But I can find out. In the meantime, I suggest we see someone more knowledgeable than me. Ask some questions. Do some more research. Then we'll see what we'll see."

"Who?" Zack and I couldn't ask fast enough.

"Why, the local pastor, of course." He crossed one leg over the other casually. "You're dealing with a demon. A devil. Something inherently evil. That's the pastor's specialty. Good versus evil."

He rose and waited for us to join him. "So I suggest we take a walk to that church you see about a block away and ask if he's in his office. If he is I suggest you tell him what you just told me."

"What can he do?"

Dennis shrugged. "I have no idea. But we'll never know if we don't ask."

Pastor Johnathon Deal turned out to be an elderly,

gray-haired widower who was also a very organized administrator. He could run a church in his sleep so he had plenty of time for us even though the summer season was coming and with it a five-fold increase in church attendance that he had to prepare for.

"What can I do for you?" he asked politely. He looked from Zack to me. "A wedding venue? This is an old-fashioned white painted church with a soaring steeple so we do get many such requests. It's picture pretty."

I turned red but Zack didn't blink and launched immediately into a description of everything that had been happening. The pastor's slight, somewhat professional smile lessened with each incident, turning into a frown that was deep and profound by the time he was done.

He turned to Dennis Penning. "What do you think, Dennis?" The two knew each other. It was why Dennis had brought us there. "You've had more to do with such things than I have. I'm the pastor of a small town church in middle America, not a missionary." He explained his friend to Zack and me. "He's been where such things happen on a regular basis if I remember correctly from the stories he's told." His raised eyebrows asked Dennis if that was right and received a slight nod. "So why me?"

Dennis steepled his fingers. "Because this is your town. Your church. Your people."

"And you think that's important? Or could become important?" He shook his head to indicate he knew nothing. "Are you looking for the help more people can provide?" His eyes narrowed. "Like an entire congregation?" He finished quietly, "A prayer chain?"

"I don't know. But there is one thing that bothers me because, no matter how I think on it, I can't figure it out. It's been bothering me ever since we saw the shimmer over the lake. I wonder why this particular evil came here. To Lewiston instead of some other town." He leaned back in his sturdy, wooden chair. "What or who brought it here? And why?"

"And you're hoping I know." The pastor's eyes turned reflective. "As far as I know, there is no reason to choose one place because isn't evil everywhere? All the time?"

"In a sense, yes, but you don't find demons keeping people awake everywhere all the time. They choose their places and their times and their victims. Lexi never had a problem until she moved here but her very first night here she was attacked." He leaned forward. "Surely that means something."

The pastor and missionary looked at each other and neither Zack nor I had a clue what they were thinking. What thoughts they were sharing. What ideas. But they remained quiet. Perhaps someday we'd have an answer to Dennis Penning's question.

Zack broke the silence. "So will you help?"

Their minds returned to the room and to Zack and me. "Of course."

"What can we do?" Zack pounded a fist into his other hand. "Just tell me what to do and I'll do it." He sat up straight. "I'm a soldier and I'm good at what I do. I'll send the idiot back to wherever it came from..."

"... that would be hell..." was the pastor's quiet interjection.

"... and I'll give it an extra kick on the way down."

The pastor said, "I'm afraid it won't be that easy."

Zack drew in a long, fierce breath. "Why not?"

Dennis answered for them both. "Because the tactics that win battles in the world you know aren't the ones that will work with the demon you must fight." He gave Zack a long, appraising look. "If you choose to fight it. If you agree to do battle." He turned to me apologetically. "He doesn't have to do anything, you know. It's not his fight. He can and possibly should walk away."

CHAPTER 12

"I know that," I said in a very small voice because of course he was right. It was my fight and mine alone. I'd gotten so used to Zack being with me that I'd almost forgotten that fact.

Dennis' next look said what he was about to say was important but he spoke as gently as possible. "If he loses, you won't be the only one losing a soul. Zack will forfeit his as well."

"No!" I was horrified. "He can't do it, then."

Zack spoke over me. "I'll do it." He turned to me. "Of course I will. No question about it."

"It's your life, Zack. Your soul. I can't ask that of you. Of anyone."

His eyes met mine and the other men in the room faded into nothingness. "It's your soul, too, Lexi, and nothing and no one, demon or otherwise, will take it from you. Not if I can help it."

He turned back to the others who'd been listening quietly. "So if you can just show me how it's done, then I'll get on it right away because the sooner we rid the world of this idiot demon, the better."

"You don't doubt your ability." The pastor looked Zack up and down and I knew what he saw. A former

soldier, muscular, large and capable, who'd been tested in battle and knew his own
strengths.

I'd benefited from those strengths in the middle of the night when the demon – and now I knew he was a demon -- whispered and Zack defended me. He was totally unafraid. Intelligent. Even more important, I suspected, he knew how to use his anger, a skill honed over years in the service. He knew how to channel his anger. To turn it into a weapon. I was pretty sure that was what he'd done when the demon taunted me

But would that be enough?

Then Dennis said one more thing that made my stomach curdle. "If you're going to do it there's no time to waste. We must get busy. I'll do some research. Contact some people I used to know who can tell us what you must do. What you must learn." His lips pressed together in a straight line. "It's urgent because now that the demon knows Zack has joined the fight it'll speed up its own timeline accordingly."

"What are you saying?"

"Demons weaken their prey to make them easier to dispatch. Usually there's no hurry but now that the demon after Lexi's soul knows you are on to it, Zack, it will work harder and faster to make Lexi weak. Make her afraid. Make her vulnerable, with the goal of taking her before you can learn how to keep her safe."

He gripped the sides of his chair as he leaned towards Zack. His knuckles were white. "It will keep after her until she can't fight any longer. You must defeat it before she grows too weak and, mark my words, each day starting today will see her grow weaker as the demon goes after what it wants." He held Zack's attention. "So we must get on it with whatever we're going to do and we must do it as soon as possible."

"If that's the case, what can I do today? Immediately?" Zack was taut, tense, ready to charge into battle. His nostrils flared, the muscles on his arms clenched, his entire being turned into something I'd not seen before. Something awesome.

The pastor brought us back to reality. "You can't do anything yet. Not until we get more information and Dennis and I will get on that right away." The two men looked from Zack to me. "For the moment, go home. Enjoy life. Sleep well each night, which you will be able to do because there will be two of you when the demon taunts Lexi. Taunt it right back when it tries to keep you awake and then sleep soundly for the rest of the night because you both need lots of rest. When we come back with more information you must be both rested and ready."

Dennis said one more thing before we left. His look met mine. "You've already made the first and most important step towards defeating the demon, Lexi." We paused. Waited because we couldn't imagine what he was talking about. "When the demon first came there was just you. Just Lexi. Now there are two of you. Lexi and Zack. Together you can do what one person can't do alone. You'll be able to rest and prepare because there are two of you and you are together."

The pastor said quietly, "An entire army would be my preference."

Zack nodded. "I know what you mean. I was once part of an army and numbers make a difference. An army can do what one person can't."

"Exactly." He waved us out of the room. "But

don't worry. That army will come into existence. There will be soldiers. They won't be the usual type of soldiers, of course, but I promise you that when the time comes, they will be ready." He took a deep breath and seemed to be looking beyond us. Beyond the room. "When the demon attacks, an army will stand with you."

Dennis finished for them both, sounding like a Shakesperean actor reciting lines. "I never thought to say this but I find that I am." He took a deep breath and slowly, deeply, said, "It is begun."

He didn't want to be there, didn't want to be involved, had seen and possibly been involved in too many similar situations, but he couldn't in good conscience ignore what was happening. I was grateful.

Zack took my hand and hauled me to my feet and towards the door. "Come on, Lexi. Like they said, there's nothing we can do now so we might as well go home where you can turn trash into treasure and I can get my house snug against the weather."

As we left, Pastor Johnathon said, "About why the demon chose Lexi. Why here. Why anything. Next time it returns and whispers in the night, why don't you ask it?"

Zack blinked and nodded. "I'll do that." In moments we were outside in the sunshine and walking beside the limpid blue lake that soon would be filled with laughing vacationers. The breeze that ruffled the surface of that lake also ruffled my hair and pressed Zack's shirt against his body and somehow, I didn't know how, the outline of that male and very competent body next to mine made me feel better. As if the whole thing was nothing more than a bad dream that would fade in the bright sunlight.

Or perhaps it was that something was being done. That I wasn't alone.

Zack turned to me calmly as if we hadn't just been discussing life and death moments earlier. "We should ask the owner of the gallery next to the café if they'll sell your stuff."

It would be wonderful to talk about something other than demons and death. "Let's see if they are open."

They weren't but the café owner said they'd said they'd be there towards the end of the afternoon so we decided to return then. We went home immediately so as to hopefully get something done that day besides discussing how to defeat demons and worrying about losing our souls.

By the time late afternoon arrived and we'd cleaned up a bit in my cottage and returned to town, Zack had closed in the walls of his house and I'd finished the reusable tote I was working on and hot glued a broken lamp back together and rewired it. All that remained was to replace the torn and dirty shade with something handmade and elegant. Easy peasy.

I took the tote and a couple boxes that I'd found at rummage sales and turned into jewelry boxes. The owners were in their store and liked what they saw. "I take it that everything you make is one-of-a-kind?" Ross Arthur turned the boxes over to the bottom where my name was wood-burned with panache. "Customers like that."

I assured him that was the case and his wife Delia said they looked forward to me bringing in more of my upcycled items and she then invited us to look through the store as they worked to make it perfect for the opening day which would be in a little over a week. "When the weather is warm enough for the water to be comfortable and vacations begin and summer people open up their cottages. Then we'll open for business."

I liked what the store had. Some high-end art, some nice craft work and some things that, like mine, didn't fit in any particular category but would appeal to the residents and visitors of Lewiston. The Arthurs had been in business enough years that they knew their customers well and I was relieved they thought my works would fit right in and would sell well. "It's the upcycled nature of what you do that's the draw. People want that."

We wandered the aisles, eventually stepping through an archway and into a back room where the high-end art was on display with each piece given proper importance and isolated from everything else. The Arthurs knew how to display art to best advantage.

As we walked among the display my stomach turned nauseous. It was sudden and bad. I grew dizzy and stopped walking. Zack, beside me, put an arm around me. "What's wrong?"

"I don't know. I don't feel good."

His eyes showed concern. "Is it the demon?" In a low voice so the Arthurs wouldn't hear.

"I don't think so." I searched my body to pinpoint how I felt. "Though it feels similar to when the demon comes."

"Let's get you out of here." He started to pull me back to the main part of the store but before we reached the arched opening that separated that room from the rest of the store, the sensation disappeared.

"I'm okay now." I pulled free and straightened my shirt where Zack had held me. "It must have been just a momentary thing." I looked back at the art we hadn't seen yet. "And I'd like to stay here a bit longer and see what they have. Some of this stuff is quite good."

So we returned to peruse the art we hadn't yet gotten around to inspecting and I felt quite good. Until suddenly I didn't. I doubled over and once more Zack held me and moved me towards the main part of the store. And once more, when we approached the store itself the sick feeling dissipated.

I straightened and Zack and I stared at one another until Zack said, "You're not sick. It's this room that's doing it to you. Or something in here." His look roved about the room, pausing on each work of art and then moving on. "It's happened twice. Each time you were standing near a similar picture." He stepped close to one of the pictures his gaze had settled on.

They were dark and brooding, modern art with a few bold slashes of color that could have represented anything or nothing. I followed his look and moved towards the picture he was looking at. I doubled over and couldn't move away fast enough.

I leaned against Zack, regaining my balance. "It could have been a coincidence."

"It wasn't." Zack pulled me once more towards the main part of the store.

"I want to make sure." I went back towards the dark pictures, a different one this time but clearly by the same artist. And the same thing happened again. This time I let Zack pull me into the main part of the store where we found the Arthurs looking at us oddly. In a worried voice, Ross Arthur asked, "Is there a problem?"

What to say? In a calm and measured tone of voice, Zack said, "Those pictures. The dark ones. They seem to upset Lexi." He held their attention as I struggled back to normal. "Who does them?"

Ross Arthur looked past us into the high-end art room. His brows knitted. "I know the ones you mean." He looked at me kindly. "You aren't the only one affected by Cameron's work. It's happened before. I almost wish we didn't sell them but some people like them." He shrugged. "I don't particularly care for them either though Cameron is obviously a gifted artist."

Zack perused the dark canvases once more. "He should get his mind out of the gutter and put a little light in his art."

The Arthurs agreed and Zack and I left. "At least those disgusting pictures aren't in the main part of the store. You can avoid them." And we went home.

To my cottage, of course, because I had the power and water that were payment for Zack helping me elude a demon that wanted my soul. Not a fair exchange, I definitely got the better of the bargain, but I was simply glad he was there as we pulled into the yard and finished the day on the deck overlooking the lake, eating left over spaghetti and garlic bread while drinking warm Coke because we'd forgotten to put any in the refrigerator before heading to town and the cottage refrigerator didn't have an ice maker.

CHAPTER 13

The demon whispered again that night. It was the darkest part of the night when the moon had set and the sun hadn't yet sent exploratory fingers through the treetops. The whisper was self-assured. As if we were old friends.

"Lexi."

I sat up immediately, pulled awake by the memory of the other nights when it had terrorized me. Yes, that was the proper term. I'd been terrified by that sound. But I wasn't now because Zack was nearby and two knowledgeable men were going to help. "Go away!"

I didn't have to pretend anger, the feeling rising through me was very real and unafraid. Okay, I wasn't afraid because of Zack in the next room, probably propped on an elbow listening because that was how he'd been the other nights when the demon had whispered. That mental picture of him sent fear scurrying away. I was full of confidence. My voice was clear. "And don't bother me again."

The whisperer laughed. The demon – because we now knew that's what the whisperer was – laughed a second time and this laugh was louder. Nastier. "Oh, dear Lexi, you are so amusing. You pretend to be so brave."

The laugh ended and the whisper turned simply evil. "But I know you, Lexi. I know your type. Kind. Loving. Trusting. But not brave. Not even a tiny bit brave. So your bravery isn't yours at all. It's the bravery of the man in the other room. What's his name? You didn't tell me his name, Lexi. I should know his name, it's only polite, because he's included in our conversations now."

"My name is Zackary Slater and I suggest you leave now and never return," came a measured, totally male voice from the other room. Loud enough to be heard but not a shout because that would signal lack of control and Zack was totally in control. Of himself. Of everything. "Because I'm getting a tad tired of the way you're bothering my friend."

"Lexi. Use her name, Zackary, it's good manners. She's our little Lexi, yours and mine at the moment, but she's going to belong to me eventually. Just me." The whisper went silent for a moment, then continued. "When I choose to take her. And you, of course, because the two of you have become a package deal."

Another menacing silence was followed by, "I look forward to devouring her lovely self. I'm sure it will be delectable. Yours, not so much, but good enough." There was a whispered sigh, long and slow. "I'm normally not in a hurry but you two are making me impatient. I want my little Lexi so I think I'll move my timeline up a bit. Wear her down. Make her vulnerable to my -- charms. Not tonight but soon, dear Lexi. Soon. And you, Zackary, will follow soon after."

Zack lost patience. He forgot to project self-control. He bellowed. "Go away, you idiot! Leave Lexi alone!" He started to bellow still more but suddenly the demon was gone and the night was just another dark night as I sat in my bed and tried to stop trembling and failed completely.

I spent the rest of the night in Zack's arms because I wouldn't have slept at all if he'd left me alone and he knew that. So he rocked me until I sagged against him, exhausted. I woke somewhat when he carefully lay me on one side of the bed and himself on the other but close enough to keep an arm around me because he knew I'd not sleep otherwise. And so we spent the hours until dawn and, surprisingly, we woke refreshed.

"Got more stuff to take to town?" Zack asked over pancakes and sausage, stuffing himself because that was how he ate, in large bites, enjoying every one. "They open in a week. You should get as much stuff to them as possible so it'll be there for potential buyers to see and fall in love with."

"You flatter me."

"I like your stuff."

"You don't even know what to call it. You just call it 'stuff.'"

"Names don't matter. It's great. Some is useful, some just lovely. No fancy label needed." He rose, his plate empty. "The morning is passing. We'd best get going."

"What about your house? You need to get it closed in."

He scratched his head. "I'm kind of stopped. For the moment, anyway." He sat back down. "All I need to get it closed to the weather is to get the windows in. But they are huge windows, heavy, and I don't want to drop them and break them." He huffed. "I'm only one person so not sure how I'll do it. Yet." He stood up once more and indicated I should too. "It'll take a bit of figuring out and I can do that while we take your stuff to town."

"I can help with the windows and we can go to town later."

"No you can't. You're a little thing and those windows require large men. Preferable several of them and I can't afford new windows if we drop them."

"Then we'll go to town like you suggested. I'll drive while you think." Because of course we'd both go. The only time we were apart now was when he worked on his house and I worked on my business and since I moved my business into his workshop we were always close. I'd probably go into withdrawal if we were apart for any length of time. I'd gotten that used to Zack in my life.

More than that, I'd gotten used to Zack himself. Zack the man. The size of him. His off-tune songs. His smiles that lit up the world. The way he moved as he worked, like a perfectly tuned and powerful machine. He was awesome. And he was about to become a demon killer.

The Arthurs liked what I brought. Driftwood from the beach in front of my cottage with beachy things hot-glued to them. Not useful at all but the Arthurs said tourists would love them. A sample of the chairs we'd found earlier that Zack had repaired and I had refinished and recovered. "Bring them all. Someone will want them for their cottage. They have the perfect vacation vibe."

"I can make a table to go with them," Zack offered.

Delia Arthur considered the chairs. "Let's see how

they go without a table. If they don't sell, then that's a good idea." She grinned. "But I doubt you'll be making a table."

We showed the Arthurs the rest of the things we'd brought and they wanted them all. I was walking on air. My new business looked like it would be exactly what I'd hoped and I hadn't even gotten around to selling online because I'd not yet figured the cost of shipping. I waltzed towards the door with Zack following. I felt his grin and knew he'd suggest coffee and donuts at the café next door. I just knew it.

Then I doubled over and held my stomach as an attack of nausea hit. Zack was beside me in seconds, holding me, pulling me to him and looking around for what must have triggered the same kind of nausea that had bothered me during our earlier trip. Except we weren't in the art gallery part of the store. We were near the back exit because the store was still closed to the public and the front door was locked.

Someone pushed that door open from the outside. A tallish, thin man with ink black hair that was longer than I cared for stepped through. He was carrying a rather large picture wrapped in brown paper. I couldn't see the picture itself but I didn't have to. I knew what it would be. Another dark, brooding modern art depiction of nothing recognizable with slashes of color that wouldn't lighten it up at all.

"Hi." The man carrying the picture paused and smiled. "Are you guys vendors too?" I nodded as best I could in the grips of nausea that grew worse as he neared us. "What do you do? Art? Craft? Something else?" Then he frowned and peered at me carefully. "Are you all right? You don't look so good."

He was being polite. I tried to respond in kind but Zack held me tight and I felt his animosity towards the man and what he carried. "It's your picture. All of your pictures. They do something to her. They make her sick."

The man's eyebrows rose but he immediately hurried his picture into the art gallery where he carefully leaned it against the wall and then returned, giving me a concerned look. "Well, that's a shock. I know my works aren't for everyone but to my knowledge this is the first time they made someone sick." He smiled tentatively. Politely. "And here I thought I was a pretty good artist. Guess I'd better work harder."

"It's probably the paint," I said through gritted teeth. "An allergy. I'm sure that's what it is."

Zack asked, "Do you use some unusual kind?"

The man shook his head. "Nope. Acrylics. Nothing special." He looked me over. "But something is definitely bothering you."

With the picture gone I felt better. Not normal but not as sick, though the other times the paintings had bothered me I'd returned to normal as soon as I got away from them. Not now, which meant it had something to do with the artist. But of course the artist would have traces of whatever he used on the pictures on his person. It only made sense.

"I'm okay now." I stayed against Zack's body and his arms remained around me because he sensed that I wasn't okay at all.

Zack didn't like the man. I felt it in his body against mine, in his arms, in his breath that hadn't speeded up in the least as he asked, not very politely,

"Why do you paint such depressing pictures?"

The man smiled. "Because some people pay a lot of money for such paintings. I like money and the more the better." He shrugged. "So who cares if they are dark and gloomy. They don't hang in my house. I don't have to look at them."

Zack shuddered but I suspected the man with the long, dark hair didn't see it. I only knew because I felt it as the man continued, holding out a hand. "My name is Cameron Blackwell and I'm glad to meet you."

Zack reluctantly introduced us and we shook hands. As soon as possible Zack backed me away from Cameron Blackwell and said we had errands to run so had to leave. He duck-walked me through the back door and into the bright day and the faint nausea disappeared completely. Sensing that I was okay, Zack released me.

I turned around to see him and almost laughed at the look on his face. "Oh Zack. He was a nice guy. He just happens to paint ugly pictures is all and I don't believe for one second that story about just using acrylics. He mixes something in with the acrylics and that something bothers me. That's all there is to it."

"I hope so." Zack muttered more things that I didn't get as he shepherded me towards the café and the coffee and donuts I knew were on his mind. "But I'll tell you the truth, Lexi. The guy bothers me and it's not just his pictures. It's him."

"Why? How?"

"I don't know. I just know he's like a bad smell that won't go away no matter how long you leave your door open." He ordered and we took our coffee and donuts outside and chose a table overlooking the lake that was growing warmer by the day thanks to the sun beating down like a furnace. "But he's gone and, hopefully, you won't have to see him or talk to him ever again."

At which moment Cameron Backstone exited the Arthur's store. Zack tensed, fearing he'd join us. But he didn't. He merely waved and smiled. In that smile was the acknowledgement that we'd not had any errands to run if we were enjoying coffee and donuts. But he continued to wherever he was heading instead of confronting us and soon disappeared around a building as Zack slid down in his chair, red-faced because he'd been caught in a lie.

"Thank you for helping me back there." I wanted him to know I didn't care that he'd lied. He'd done it for me.

"No problem."

"You don't have to do this, you know. This whole thing. Whispers in the night and pictures that make me sick. It's way more than either of us thought would happen when we made an agreement. Demons and souls and such weren't even on the docket."

"I'm not going anywhere."

"Are you sure?" I held his look. Stared at him. Tried to read his thoughts because a soul is a valuable thing and he was putting his on the line for me.

"I'm sure." He met my look full on. I wished I could read that look but there were too many things swirling in his China blue eyes for me to pick out just one. Our gazes held for a long time, until a gull swooped down to check for left-over donuts, chasing us away from the table and into the rest of the day.

CHAPTER 14

Zack didn't get his windows in that day. He scowled. "I need a block and tackle."

"What's that?"

"A big thing I'll have to make."

"Will it take long?"

"Yep." He looked depressed. A first for the man with endless self-confidence.

"Are you sure I can't help? It would save time."

He was horrified. "I'll not let you near my very expensive, triple glazed, picture windows."

"Okay,"

My reply was so meek that he relented. "I didn't mean to belittle you, Lexi. But you must admit you aren't the largest person and I don't see bulging muscles anywhere on you."

"I just want to help."

"You are helping by being you. By caring. By being with me."

I turned red but couldn't stop grinning at the compliment. Then Zack did something unexpected. With a grin of his own that matched mine, he swooped down and kissed me.

We'd not come even close to kissing before but what happened next wasn't a platonic kiss on the cheek, nor was it a friendly peck. It was a major kiss, the kind that sent my body into overdrive and made me think I'd been right about there being more to this relationship than I'd dared admit to my reflection in the mirror every morning.

If it was real then it was what I'd hoped for all along while telling myself I didn't care because I hadn't thought there was any possibility he'd feel what I'd been feeling ever since seeing him singing away on the other side of our mini forest. I was left breathless as he released me and finished with, "Thank you for reminding me there are wonderful people in the world willing to help and that the future lies ahead, bright and full of a million possibilities for both of us."

What did he mean by 'both of us?' Was he referring to two separate individuals who deserved to be happy in our own separate lives? Or did he mean both of us together? As in a couple? I didn't have a clue but wondering kept my mind busy for the rest of the day as I sat on the deck of my cottage and mapped out what to do with some of the things I'd gathered from dumpsters. As I pondered junk, Zack went online in the office alcove to learn how to build a block and tackle. Whatever that was.

Getting his house closed in would take longer than planned. It was a setback. But it would get done eventually, of that I was sure because anything Zack attempted, he accomplished. As I watched him frown in concentration as he stared at a picture of a block and tackle on the computer, I could only hope demon slaying would soon be a thing of the past.

He made me hopeful about keeping my soul and it was only then, knowing there was hope, that I realized I'd expected the worst ever since that first demon whisper, even before knowing what it was after, just that it was evil.

But it wasn't just Zack that made me feel better. The pastor also had said the demon wasn't all-powerful. Putting everything together I realized that optimism had been creeping into me ever since Zack came into my life and that optimism had grown after meeting the pastor and his missionary friend.

I went to bed that night knowing that if and when the demon chose to whisper more threats, Zack would be there. In person. With me. For me. Helping me do what I now knew was possible. Defeating a demon from Hell. And the pastor and missionary would be with us during the battle.

The demon did come that night, during the darkest hours when the air was black as coal and the night birds went silent. It was their silence that told me it was in the room with me and I wouldn't have to wait long to hear its evil voice. And I didn't.

It whispered as it always did. "Lexi." A pause, then, "Are you awake, lovely Lexi? Are you listening? Were you waiting eagerly for my voice?" Followed by its usual deprecating laugh.

I didn't get a chance to answer because Zack was beside me before I could say a word. "Leave her alone, you idiot! I told you before to stop bothering her and I'm losing patience so I'll just say it once more. Leave Lexi Tremaine alone."

"Or what?" The demon cackled softly. "What will you do, you poor, ineffectual man? You pathetic human."

"I'm pathetic?!" Scorn dripped from Zack's tongue. "You're the one that's pathetic. You don't even show yourself. You hide in the night. You're a coward. You're afraid."

The whisper grew louder. Angrier. "I'm not afraid of anything, least of all you, a mere mortal." Its boast was clear in its next words. "Be grateful, human, that I'm letting you live. For now." The next whisper was smooth as oil and just as toxic. "Because you don't appeal to me."

So perhaps the pastor was wrong. Perhaps Zack's soul wasn't in danger. But the demon's next words dashed that hope. "But perhaps I should take you now anyway and destroy your soul completely. I should do the world a favor and it rid of one more human. Perhaps I'll send your soul directly to Hell instead of consuming those delectable parts of you. I'll let devils play with it for eternity and I'll choose the time for you to die for no other reason than because I can. And because you annoy me."

"You're so full of it! I'm a human and I scare you but you're too afraid to admit it!" Zack's taunt was full of laughter. "A mere human scares you. Me. But actually that's only right. You should be afraid of me because I can beat the pants off you." He laughed again, loudly and with the brazen self-confidence I'd learned was a part of him. "I don't believe you can do anything at all. You're just a powder puff." The taunt hung in the dark.

The dark around us changed. It became charged. It grew. It turned malevolent. Sparks rent the air, sending electricity through the bedroom though nothing could be seen. It was black lightning in a black room. "You doubt me, Zackary Slater, but you shouldn't."

"I not only doubt you, I dare you to show yourself."

"Never doubt me, little man," came the whisper, once more low and oily. The demon had lost control for a moment but now had it back. "If you saw me you couldn't stand the brilliance that is me. You'd curl up and die." A chuckle followed, evil and full of self-pride. "But though I won't show you my real self I'll show both of you what I can do. Not much, you understand, because that would be impossible for two puny humans to deal with."

There was silence for a moment. I felt the demon thinking. Then deciding something. "I'm not ready to take Lexi yet. Soon, but not tonight." There was a silence during which I thought it might have left until it continued, "But tomorrow you'll see a small example of my power. In the morning."

"What are you talking about? You never come during the day. Because you're a coward as well as an idiot." Zack was eager. He couldn't wait to meet the demon and I could feel him looking forward to whatever the demon would do. Something tangible he could battle and defeat.

"Oh don't worry, you won't see me. I'd not want to overwhelm you with my amazing self. Instead I think I'll start small. But it's time I start getting Lexi ready to be mine."

"What will you do?" Zack tried to keep up the bravado that had come easily so far but there was a tinge of concern in his words and the demon heard it.

Another chuckle was followed by, "In the morning

when she wakes up, Lexi will know how powerful I am. She'll know she belongs to me. Because she will be weak. It'll be hard for her to function. She'll be helpless."

"Never. And if she is a bit tired, I'm here for her." Zack added, "There are two of us, you sick thing, and together we can defeat anything, even idiot demons that think they are all powerful."

Another laugh. "Good luck with that, Zackary Slater. No one can help her. I'm going to make her mine. To take her life force and send her soul to Hell. Yes, Zackary Slater, she will feed me. She will become a part of me. Willing or otherwise." Still another laugh. "And there's nothing you can do about it."

"You…!" Zack stopped mid-sentence because the demon was gone. Just like that. We knew it more by the feel of the air than anything substantial. The dark was once more just normal dark and the night birds once again sang their songs. And I curled in fear, afraid of what the morning would bring.

"Don't believe it," Zack said beside me, holding me, rocking me, making me know I was safe with a sureness that was deeper than words. "That stupid demon can do his best but I'm better than any whisper in the night and I'll keep you safe." He tipped my head up slightly and I felt rather than saw the intensity of him. "I promise, Lexi, that you'll be safe. And I always keep my promises."

He kissed me again but this time there was no man-woman heat. Instead it was all comfort and peace and the feel of it settled into my flesh and I raised my face to better take in what he was giving and I melded with him even though it was just a kiss. Or two. Or three.

Then he murmured, "If you become one with anyone, it'll be me. No one else. Not now, not ever." But there was a question in his voice. He was asking if his kisses had gone too far.

"Yes," was my instant answer. "It'll be us. Together." And he gathered me closer and we sat that way for what seemed like forever and was probably just long enough to fall asleep.

The next day was Sunday and the morning was bright and clear. I woke, stretched and wished Zack was still beside me. He wasn't but I heard his off-key song in the kitchen so I snuggled deeper beneath the quilt and thought ahead to another of his wonderful breakfasts. Zack was a food guy and breakfast was the first meal of the day. He did it well. So I closed my eyes and dreamed of pancakes and sausage.

"Wake up, sleepy-head." It wasn't much later and the smell of breakfast made my mouth water. He shook the quilt and pulled it off my face enough that he could see I was awake. I blinked at him, remembered what he'd said during the night, and turned red and hoped he didn't notice. He did. "No more sleeping in." That's what his words said. His eyes said he remembered those kisses and wondered how we should proceed.

I rolled over and stretched. And fell back onto the bed, surprised that I didn't want to get up. "I'm tired."

I tugged at the quilt but he didn't let go of it. "You slept well. I know. I was there."

"I'm still tired. More than tired. Exhausted." I expanded on my statement. "I feel like I ran a race and collapsed at the finish line."

Frown lines appeared "The demon said—" He stopped.

"That I'd be tired this morning."

Our looks met, his full of concern and something else in those flecks that turned his eyes elemental and whatever it was passed mere concern and continued on into life and death. Those eyes probed deeply into mine while I avoided thinking. I was too tired.

Without another word, Zack pulled the quilt off and hauled me upright. "That's it, Lexi. Time to get up." Casually, as if it was just me being lazy and we'd both laugh about it later, he swung my legs over the side of the bed and dropped onto the bed beside me, holding me gently, supporting me in case I fell.

But I didn't. The day began pouring into me through the open window and the weariness dissipated enough for me to take charge of myself. "I'm good now. I can take it from here. I don't know what got into me but it's gone now. Mostly."

"If you're sure." As much a question as a statement and I was grateful he didn't repeat what the demon had whispered in the night. It would have been too much to deal with. "I'll get breakfast on the table."

CHAPTER 15

"It's Sunday." Zack's look cornered me as I finished the last pancake and prepared to shove away from the table with a satisfied groan.

"So?"

"So Sunday is church day." He amended that with, "It's church day for people who choose to go." His eyebrows rose in question. "Do you go to church?"

I slumped. "Not as often as I should."

"Me neither."

We stared at one another until he said, "Maybe today is the day to start."

I rose, fighting the weariness that remained, the odd and unusual tinge of exhaustion that the bright day couldn't dispel. "Because the people who know about demons will be there. In the pulpit. In the congregation. Spilling into the aisles."

Church would be an acknowledgement of what was happening. That a demon from Hell wanted my soul. I couldn't believe how hard it was to admit such a thing. To give credence to the unbelievable. To face a danger I'd never in my wildest imaginings dreamed I'd have to deal with.

Zack held out a hand and took mine. It was large

and strong and warm and exactly what I needed. It suddenly occurred to me that without Zack I'd already have given up. My soul would be forfeit. With him, I'd fight with everything in me. I had a chance. I looked squarely at him and said, "Let's go to church."

We got there just in time to slide into the back pew as the service started. But even in the back, even being almost late, the pastor recognized us. He didn't nod or do anything obvious, but his gaze roving over the congregation stopped when it reached us. Paused for a time. And continued on as if nothing had caught his interest, but we knew differently and that difference was evident after the service when people strolled to another room where coffee and cookies were available to everyone who wanted some. Which was everyone, including us.

"Chocolate chip." Zack, the food guy, tasted one cookie and his eyes lit up. "Got to get the recipe."

"Do you bake?"

"No but maybe I should learn. A new skill for my after-military life."

"I'll bake a batch of cookies for you."

"Will you do that? Really? What payment will you take?"

"Defeat of one demon." I meant my comment to be facetious. Instead it landed between us like a lump of lead as the pastor came to our table and sat across from us. We were the only ones at the table and when an elderly couple headed our way to be sociable, an almost unnoticeable shake of his head sent them elsewhere. He wanted to talk to us alone and without interruption and they understood.

He swirled his coffee. "Demons. And Hell." He

soke mildly and took a sip. "Two interesting topics."

Zack was blunt. "It returned last night. It's started its campaign for Lexi's soul." His eyes narrowed until the two of us and the pastor were the only ones in the room. "This morning Lexi was so exhausted she could hardly move which was exactly as the demon said would happen, a way to make her know its power."

Pastor Johnathon nodded as still more people came to our table with cups of coffee but these people ignored his frown. They sat and nibbled cookies and gave Zack and me interested looks because we were newcomers. It was the end of privacy.

The pastor leaned back, sighed softly, and said quietly, "Later. Mind if I visit you guys this afternoon? I'll ask Dennis if he'll come, too, since he's the resident expert on your particular problem." Not mentioning demons specifically because by then we were surrounded by half a dozen congregants who'd ask questions we didn't want to answer.

They were nice people with the usual polite questions asked of newcomers. Who were we? Where were we from? Were we just visiting or did we plan on staying? The last question got a response from Zack. "I'm staying and I'll have a house to prove it as soon as I get some huge windows installed that I might not have bought if I'd have known how hard they would be to move into place."

That brought questions about his house and how much progress he'd made so far. And about the windows in question and how he proposed to get them where they needed to be. One of the newcomers, a middle aged man with a soft, comfortable stomach spoke. "Want some help?"

Zack didn't know how to answer. The man obviously wouldn't be any more help than I'd be but he ignored Zack's polite scowl that was designed to put him off as he said, "There's lots of teenaged boys around here with not enough to do. Seems to me that hauling a few windows around will keep them out of trouble and help them build muscles to show off."

The pastor agreed. "I'll remind them they are supposed to do good deeds." He smiled "Their parents will approve and later maybe will let them do more of the dumb things they want to do because they actually did this one helpful thing."

I remembered my teenaged years. "I'll feed them. Pop and pizza and snacks. And since the house is on the lake, they can go swimming later." I shuddered. "If the water is warm enough."

The man with the soft paunch set his cup down. "What better way to show off than by carrying heavy things and if the water is too cold they'll never admit it if there are teenaged girls around."

"Are there teenaged girls who'll come and motivate them?"

The pastor smiled broadly. "Of course there are. I'll get right on it. And find a few chaperones."

Two hours later, cars and trucks showed up at Zack's house with enough teenaged boys to hoist the windows into place and hold them there safely while Zack and an army of middle-aged men secured them. It went so smoothly I almost didn't have food ready by the time they were done.

But I managed and the rest of the afternoon was spent watching teenaged boys jump off a pontoon boat that had magically appeared while teenaged girls watched and either screamed whenever they were splashed or joined the boys in the cold water.

But no one swam for long. The water was still too cold for that and, eventually, everyone left. Except Pastor Johnathon and the missionary, Dennis Penning.

We were seated around the picnic table that had been in front of Zack's tent until he moved in with me and moved it beside the workshop. I stared at the huge windows that would give Zack a magnificent view of the lake and also of the woods to one side. Though the inside was bare the house looked finished from the outside, needing only paint, and, more importantly, it was tight to the weather. "It'll be an awesome house," I said, looking at the lovely picture windows.

"It will indeed," he answered with a contented burr in his voice. "And I look forward to many years of staring through those very large windows while drinking coffee and eating those chocolate chip cookies you promised."

He tipped his head and added, low enough that only I could hear, "Which, if I have my way, just might be made in the kitchen at the back of my house that you'll see when we go inside to check out the view through the new windows." He reached for me. "And, by the way, I promise the kitchen will also have great views and will be perfect for any and all cooking and baking. Wouldn't have it any other way."

Would I ever use that kitchen? It sounded like Zack wanted me to. Or would I be in Hell? I deliberately shut off that thought as he took my hand and rubbed a thumb across my wrist as I said, "Your house is now closed to the weather." He agreed so I continued. "It's a milestone. You can move in and start living. You can finish the inside without worrying about rain or anything."

"You're right about that. I can move in. But I'd rather not. Not yet." He pulled me around to see him better. "Not until this demon thing is dealt with." As if it was nothing special and slaying demons was an every-day occurrence. "Until then, I'll stick to you like glue. If you'll allow it."

"That's a good idea." We'd forgotten the pastor and missionary who were now looking at us with speculative expressions that could have been because we were giving out vibes as a couple or because, now that the windows were in and the workers gone, it was time to discuss a demon from Hell.

Dennis Penning put his hands between his knees and began. "I contacted some people I worked with when I was a roving missionary. Africa. The far east. People everywhere still believe in demons and they do so with good reason."

"Do they know how to fight them?" Zack's voice was lazy but the undertone was deadly serious.

Dennis nodded. "There are many ways. Many techniques. But the main thing is that the techniques aren't what defeats demons. They are merely ways to find that something inside of you that can defeat them. The fire in the belly. The heat of righteousness. Because that's the only thing that will send them away and, hopefully, eliminate them entirely."

"A demon can be totally eliminated? As in killed?" Zack's brow furrowed. "But they aren't alive."

"Not in the sense we know. But they can be defeated. They can cease to exist. It's difficult but not impossible." He shrugged. "All of which is esoteric information and not important at the moment. All that matters today is that you find a way to focus. To fan the fire in your belly until it's hot enough to defeat even a demon from Hell."

The pastor had remained silent. Now he spoke. "Do those things make sense to you? Focus? Fire in the belly? Because if it doesn't, we'll have to rethink this whole demon thing. If you can't focus or if you simply don't know what we're talking about, then don't even try. Because you'll fail."

Zack smiled. "Focus always makes the difference in war. Weapons are necessary. Strategy is crucial. But the thing that wins battles is mental. What you call a fire in the belly. Focus and determination and knowing you are in the right."

Dennis got a far-away look in his eyes. "That's it. That's what all those so-called primitive people knew that we so-called civilized people tend to forget. That it's in the will to win. And in the mind. And the heart."

They'd been talking over and around me. Now I spoke up. "I can't believe it's that simple."

Dennis turned to me. "Those things aren't everything. Of course they aren't. But they are the important things. The rest is details and I'll do more sleuthing to find out about those details. How, exactly, to fight demons. Techniques. Weapons. Armor. And whatever else is required."

A thrill went along my spine. It was coming together. An awesome battle. A fight to the finish. A war Zack would win. No other possibility existed. I couldn't allow myself to think of anything other than victory, though my stomach wanted to regurgitate everything I'd consumed that day and only fierce concentration on the men before and beside me and the peaceful lake beyond could make it stay down.

Dennis Penning rose and Pastor Johnathon followed. "Time for us to go. We've got lots to do. People to consult. Information to process."

The pastor said, "And I've got a congregation to care for." He nodded to Zack and me. "Including you two."

They left but Zack and I stayed at the picnic table for hours, watching the sun drop below the horizon, listening to the day birds go to sleep and the night birds come out, feeling the air cool as shadows lengthened. Eventually, Zack sighed and rose, then he held out his hand to me and I rose, too, much as Pastor Jonathon had done with Dennis Penning.

"Time to get some sleep." He paused, then gave a wry grin. "In spite of the demon. It will come tonight because it's now counting down the time till it thinks it'll get you. Which it won't. Ever." He pulled me close. "Because when it comes, I'll be there, waiting and ready. And I'll let it know it'll have to go through me to get to you."

CHAPTER 16

The demon did come again that night – of course it did -- and, as promised, Zack was beside me when it manifested, one arm around me, heart beating normally, breathing steady, unafraid and ready to confront it. Eager, even. That eagerness thrummed so strongly I feared that merely because we were touching I'd be electrocuted. Or at least burned. In a good way.

There was no whisper when the demon showed up. Not at first. We knew, though, that it was there. We'd learned to sense it. The room was suddenly darker than dark, the silence lethal and the air stifling with a faint scent of sulfur. The scent I'd not recognized until I learned the whisperer was a demon from Hell.

Zack went on the offensive, speaking before the demon had a chance. "I've said it before and I'll say it again. Leave. Lexi. Alone." His arm tightened around me. I was sure it wasn't intentional. It was merely Zack being Zack. Tough. Dominant. Self-assured. "Go away, you coward."

Whispered laughter answered him. Waves of laughter. "Puny human. You think you are my equal." More laughter, followed by a sibilant hiss, like that of a snake. "But you aren't. You saw my power this morning and that was just a small demonstration. An after-thought and done with no effort."

More laughter followed, more hissing, more pure evil that turned the black night into something other than night. It became a suffocating, stifling, putrid thing that was alive yet not alive and was followed by an unexpected silence and then another whisper. "But enough for now."

There was a pause during which the air grew so thick I thought I'd not be able to breathe. "I came tonight to check on Lexi. My Lexi. I won't take her tonight. I'll let her live a while longer and think about me. About belonging to me. But I'll check back tomorrow night to see how she's coming. How weak she is. How compliant. Perhaps I'll wait a few nights before I take her. Perhaps several. I don't know precisely when I'll take her. But it'll happen. Because Lexi is mine and nothing you do can change that."

Then, so suddenly the change was disorienting the demon was gone and the night was once more just night. The air was clear and cool. Stars glittered through the open window. Night sounds came softly. And Zack's arms around me relaxed.

"It's gone." Surprise was evident in his words. "It wasn't here long."

"Why taunt me and then just leave?"

I felt Zack's shrug and I breathed deeply of the sweet night air as he said, "It's a demon. Don't expect logic." He hugged me. "The only thing that matters is that it's gone and you can now get a good night's sleep. You've regained much of your strength after last night's demonstration, but you're still tired."

He rose, pulled the quilt over me and pushed the

hair off my forehead as if I was a child. "So go to sleep, Lexi. I'll see you in the morning and I expect you to be the bright and shiny woman I know you to be." And he was gone, moving silently but leaving behind that assurance I now knew was as natural to him as breathing.

The night went as Zack predicted. I slept deeply and woke with the sun streaming through the window, preventing me from going back to sleep, while through the closed door to the bedroom an off-key voice I'd come to love sang softly to the accompaniment of footsteps in the kitchen. Zack the food guy was in full breakfast mode.

The voice I'd come to love?

Now where had that thought come from?

In a fit of honesty, I amended that musical concept somewhat. I wasn't just in love with a voice, I was in love with the guy who owned that voice and that guy was Zack. Truly in love. Top to bottom, side to side, off-key songs, total self-assurance, and every other thing about him.

I stuck my head under my pillow and groaned as I realized love had finally, irrevocably happened to me and I wondered how it had happened and wished it hadn't and was insanely glad it had.

Then, because I couldn't stay in bed all day, I threw the pillow across the room in a fit of frustration, got up, sneaked into the bathroom for a quick shower and a peek in the mirror to see if my feelings showed and then dressed and headed for the table and another Zack breakfast. It would be a gargantuan meal made by a former army guy and could probably feed an entire regiment. At least. Maybe two regiments.

After we ate and cleaned up, when Zack headed to his house in order to start working on the inside now that it was closed to the weather, I trailed after him. He turned when he realized what I was doing. "Don't you have stuff to do? Business stuff? Trash to turn into treasure? Odd pieces of nothing in particular that you'll make into things so exquisite people will fight over the chance to buy them?" Because, though I often worked in his workshop, I also loved working on my deck where the breeze came across the lake and the sun turned frothy water into diamonds and Zack had noticed that fact.

I closed the gap between us. "I could work on the deck." I reached him and we both stopped as I tried to articulate why I was there. "I probably should because I don't need your shop today. But I prefer your shop."

He placed his hands on his hips and spread his legs wide as he examined me. "Why?" Knowing the answer but wanting me to say it.

"Because the demon is getting to me and you're my safety net." There. I'd said it and I didn't look away though I was tempted because I sounded childish.

He merely nodded, took my hand, and turned us both towards the large, old house he was remodeling that, when finished, would be a place of love and laughter – I knew that for sure though I didn't know how I knew -- with views of unvarnished beauty and room enough for a family or two or three. A place that would ring with off-key songs and host breakfasts that would become legendary. If he lived long enough. If he could defeat the demon and save, not only my soul, but his own and finish that lovely house.

He didn't have to fight a demon. He didn't have to

put his soul on the line. A soul is a precious thing and you only get one. No do-overs. "Why are you doing this?" I had to know. "Why risk your soul?" Unsaid was why risk his soul for me, another person, when he could simply let me go to Hell while he stayed safe in the house he was remodeling one board at a time.

His voice was husky when he replied. "Because." He was quiet for a long time, then he repeated, "Just because." He drew me close and wrapped an arm around me. He was warm and large and solid and everything safe and I wanted to stay that way forever. But he wasn't finished. "Because it's you and me. The two of us. Together." He pulled back enough to see my expression and added a question. "Right?"

I nodded, wondering if the mirror had been wrong and my feelings did show. Whatever he saw, though, I answered honestly. "Right." My voice quavered.

His didn't. "I repeat. For the two of us. Forever." His voice dropped lower, huskier. He had to clear his throat to get the words out. "Is that okay with you?"

"Yep. Okay with me."

And we stood like that for a long time, knowing what we'd just admitted to each other, stunned that we both felt the same way. Then he swooped low enough for a quick kiss that was lightning and thunder and everything wonderful in the space of a second or two and then we continued on so he could get some work done on his house because the day was passing and it was time to get busy. "I'm thinking about plumbing today. Running water will be pure luxury."

"Do you know anything about plumbing?"

"I have a book." And endless belief in himself. It would be enough. The plumbing would be perfect.

The plumbing took a week, after which we turned faucets on and off and watched water cascade into tubs and showers and sinks and everywhere possible and then stop when we wanted it to stop because everything worked perfectly. Of course it did.

But I was tired and turned those faucets slowly. He looked at me and scowled. "You should rest."

"I'm okay."

"No you're not. The demon comes whenever it chooses. Whatever night. And every time it comes, the following morning you're more exhausted than the time before. And it's bad and getting worse." He stepped close and examined me minutely. "You can't take much more."

"I'm fine."

"No you're not." The scowl deepened. "If you get much worse than you are now, you'll disappear. Evaporate." His eyes slitted. "And the demon will have you." Those blue eyes turned darker as his lips formed a thin, angry line. "Except it won't happen. I won't let it."

I finally said what I'd been thinking lately, as I grew more and more tired. "Maybe there's no hope."

"There's always hope." He took a deep breath. "I've been talking with Dennis Penning. He's taught me a lot about demons and they are not the unbeatable things people think they are." He tipped his head one way and another to examine me better.

I knew what he saw. Shadows beneath my eyes, even though many nights I slept well. Thought I slept. Perhaps I didn't. I only knew that each morning I was more tired than the previous one. And each day I had less and less energy. Even the sun on the water no longer made me smile though the lake was now warm enough for water sports and was filled with vacationers, swimming and boating and generally enjoying themselves.

"I'm going to have a talk with that demon next time it comes." Zack's face went still and I thought of warriors of old preparing for battle. He was somewhere else mentally. I didn't know where except it was where warriors went before putting their lives on the line.

"You don't have to do this, Zack. You shouldn't. I don't want you to." Because one soul lost was bad enough. Two was unthinkable if there was an alternative. And there was and all it involved was my accepting my fate in order to save the soul of the man I loved.

"Yes I do have to do this and I am going to do it and nothing you can say or do will change that."

He left no room for argument. In some deep part of me I was glad even as another part feared for the worst for both of us. I said the only thing I could think to say. "Are you ready?"

A shadow crossed his face. "Ready enough. No one is ever totally ready to pit themselves against an enemy. You do it when the day arrives and pray you're ready and will be victorious."

Victorious. And old-fashioned word that spoke of demons and death and epic battles. I could only hope he would be victorious instead of the demon.

In the meantime, though, Zack's house needed electricity but not to worry, he had another book, this one on how to wire a house. After much careful reading and the unwinding of coils of electric wires and the drilling of many holes for those wires to go through, one day lights went on and the hot water heater worked. Of course they did. Zack had done the work and he never failed. It wasn't possible.

Or was it?

Demons weren't like houses. There were no books on demon slaying. Unless there were. Unless Dennis Penning had somehow found them and read them and was now passing on their knowledge to Zack and he was learning, just as he'd learned how to wire a house. Or how to be a soldier.

I didn't know what to do, what to think, how to feel. So I prayed. Then I prayed again. And then again. I prayed Zack would be victorious. But I also prayed that if the worst happened he would let me die, let my soul be consumed and then go on to live a long, happy life with someone else because no one, not even Zack, is perfect and I didn't want him to give up his soul for me.

I told him what I prayed for and he laughed at the very idea of losing the battle. He was committed. And sure of himself. Totally. That assurance frightened me more than anything else could. Each day I gathered Little Guy in my arms and basked in his wriggly love and told him Zack would need him if things went bad and I disappeared. He'd need a lot of puppy love.

Little Guy licked my face and assured me he'd care for the man I loved. If that man still existed after the coming battle. If he had somehow kept his soul as I lost mine.

He had to survive. He must. But evil is incredibly powerful.

CHAPTER 17

"I've had enough." Zack's arms around me were relaxed and strong as we watched the sun dip below the trees along the shore. It had been one of my favorite pastimes growing up, watching day turn into night and the sky turn pink, then red, then purple with matching reflections on the water that riffles and eddies turned into a thousand shards of color.

Not so enjoyable now, though, because night followed that display and night brought the demon. Zack sensed my thoughts and sought to reassure me. "Next time that idiot shows up whispering and sounding like a sick cow, I'm going on the offensive."

"Don't!" I was terrified.

"I'm going to do it. You can't take much more and I've learned a lot about slaying demons, thanks to Dennis Penning and Pastor Johnathon. So it's time." He hugged me a little tighter and I knew – because I knew Zack – that arguing would be futile. "Don't worry, Lexi. It'll be fine. You'll soon be free of this insanity."

The missionary and pastor had been at his house many times recently, taking advantage of the electricity so there were lights to see by and the working plumbing provided water to drink through the simple motion of turning a faucet.

Zack's house was coming together nicely. No finished interior walls yet beyond those few left intact from when the house was first built and even those were merely studs, skeletons of past rooms, but now there were also chalk lines and piles of two-by-fours to indicate where future walls would be.

Zack had moved his huge table into the house and the three men had sat around it drinking coffee and eating donuts from the bakery in town while discussing arcane topics I didn't understand. Demon stuff.

My casual eavesdropping taught me that demon slaying didn't involve the usual type of weapons. No rifles, nor the ancient crossbows that must have been prevalent when demon slaying was a normal, everyday subject of conversation instead of a reason for people to laugh at the speaker.

I learned that slaying demons was mental, a battle of wills. And of faith, according to the pastor because when things got really bad and you didn't have physical weapons waiting in reserve then faith was all you had so you'd better make sure it was there when you needed it.

"I have faith," Zack said. "Faith in my ability, even if the coming battle will be somewhat different from those I'm used to fighting." He downed a donut in one bite. "And you've taught me how to summon both mental and emotional weapons. So I'm good."

His head tipped a bit and he grinned that irrepressible grin I now knew to be an integral part of him. "And, thanks to you guys, I can turn thought into a light saber just by waving my hands." The grin grew.

"Would have come in handy a few times in my military past." He looked the pastor up and down. "So why don't soldiers use light as a weapon? I don't think I've ever seen it done."

The pastor shrugged as if the question wasn't new. "Slaying evil is a bit different from the warfighting you're used to. Demons know they are evil and always choose dark for their weapons. But where humans are concerned, everyone seems to feel their side is right and so everyone chooses light. Light cannot fight light so there's no battle."

"Interesting," was Zack's quiet comment and I suspected that he, like me, was re-evaluating everything he'd ever known about good and evil. The subject was complicated and I hoped I'd live long enough to learn more about it.

After the pastor and missionary left we watched the sun disappear below the horizon as the red and purple and pink sky became the soft black of night that somehow still allowed for silhouettes rising around us with shiny stars dotting the firmament above.

It was lovely and I didn't touch the left-over donuts Zack consumed with zeal because if I'd taken even one it would have come right back up and splattered all over the table. I was that afraid and my fear didn't lessen as the hours passed because I knew in my heart that the demon would come that night – I just knew it -- and its visit would set into motion events I dreaded and couldn't prevent no matter how much I wanted to.

It happened shortly after we went to the cottage where we still lived most of the time and headed for bed. And waited.

The waiting was so agonizing that I developed a

splitting headache. Zack rubbed my shoulders and neck while murmuring that everything would come right in the end and all he needed was for the demon to show up so he could get things started. He was ready.

Then the demon came. It was preceded by that all-enveloping dark that was blacker than black and the putrid smell that permeated everything and had a hint of sulfur, plus the odd heat that accompanied it that wasn't any kind of heat I knew that pressed on my body like a living thing. Each time the demon showed up, our surroundings grew more oppressive. More evil.

Zack straightened, unafraid. Took a deep breath. His hand dropped from my shoulder. "You!" His voice said this visit would be different. That he was taking charge. "Demon!"

"Yes?" The whisper was filled with laughter. Or the hissing that passed for it.

"You're a coward and I'm here to tell you you're toast. Worse than toast. You will soon be nothing. You'll cease to exist."

More laughter. "I find you almost interesting, human, though your feeble threats don't bother me at all. Because I've heard them before, so many times, and I'm still here and those that made the threats aren't." The hissing grew, then subsided. "Where do you think those poor souls are now?" More hissing. "Because their souls were forfeit." Silence again. "As will yours be." More silence, then, "Both of your souls."

Zack didn't flinch. Instead his body touching mine grew taut. "Demon! Hear me! I challenge you to a duel."

"A duel?" The air changed. Grew turbulent. Flashes of fire licked the walls of the bedroom without burning anything. "A real duel?" The fire subsided. "A duel could be interesting. A change of routine. A bit of fun, so to speak. But you'll lose so not as interesting at it might be if you were a worthy opponent."

"Anywhere. Any time." Zack's arms folded and he sat straighter and waited for a reply.

The demon spoke. "Truly? You're not jesting? You actually challenge me?" Silence for a moment, then, "I pity you and your pathetic girlfriend but your challenge intrigues me enough to consider it." More silence. "As a matter of fact, I find it intriguing."

The oppressive night grew darker and pressed on us harder, black with hatred and red with fire, growing and growing until suddenly it coalesced into one huge bonfire that smelled of sulfur that burned nothing as the demon said, "I accept."

"Anywhere. Any time." Zack's voice didn't waver as he laid out his conditions.

The demon's reply came almost immediately. "Here. Behind that small forest that separates your house from others. As for the time, I think a week from now. A week from tonight. That will give you time to say goodbye to those you love."

"I'll be there but there's no need to say goodbye because I'm not going anywhere. Neither is Lexi. You are, though." No increased heartbeat, no deeper breathing. Zack wasn't afraid. Instead he was merely stating a fact as he said, "Because when I'm done you won't be a demon any more. You won't be anything."

A hiss of laughter followed. "Since I chose the time and place, you get to choose the weapons." A pause, then, "I'm interested in your choice. Cannons? Nuclear devices? What?"

"Light and dark and I choose light."

Surprise was evident in the demon's next words. "Light versus dark? It's clear you've been talking with someone. But it will make no difference. In spite of your preparations, in spite of what you think will happen, you and your girlfriend will be mine and I'll take you both gladly and enjoy consuming you, piece by piece, tidbit by tidbit, while you writhe in agony. Because I won't cease to exist. You, on the other hand, will learn what everlasting fire feels like."

The dark faded. Changed and dissipated. "Until next week, then." And the night was once more just another lovely summer night and we sat on the bed without words for a long time.

Until Zack said, "One week from now you'll be free."

I turned into him and stopped thinking because such was beyond me. Instead, I felt. The air. The night. The solitary stars above. The man with his arms around me who had no fear, unlike me who was consumed with terror. The beating of his heart, steady and strong, and the in and out of his breathing that he truly believed would continue for years to come because the demon would be defeated. Piece of cake.

"I think I'll ask the pastor and Dennis Penning to come around. Not that I need them. I'm pretty sure I've learned everything they could teach about fighting evil. But it's always a good idea to double check everything."

"Tomorrow?"

"If they aren't busy."

They weren't, or if they were they rearranged their schedules. I suspected that was what they'd done but they acted casual and confident as they arrived and took their places at that huge table in Zack's half-finished house. I joined them. I couldn't stay away. I didn't want to think about death and evil and Hell but now that it was real and I couldn't avoid it, I wanted to know everything possible. Needed to know.

"There's only one more thing for you to learn. One more skill." Pastor Johnathon's voice was so casual I knew it wasn't casual at all. Dennis Penning had done most of the talking up to that point. This would be the pastor's contribution.

"What's that?" Zack was truly relaxed but alert so whatever came next would be imprinted on his brain to be recalled later if and when it was needed.

"Help. How to summon help if you run into trouble."

"Help?" Zack frowned. "There's help? By whom? And why would anyone help? It's dangerous." Unsaid was that he was a soldier so danger was his responsibility and his alone.

The pastor smiled. "Prayer."

Zack snorted. "I'll take all the prayers you care to send skyward on my account but I doubt they will be much help in the moment." He tipped his head towards the pastor. "So thanks, and please pray all you wish, but I'll rely on myself and my skills."

The pastor's smile broadened. "I was thinking along the lines of many people praying, not just me."

Zack snorted again. "Not likely. Won't happen. The minute you tell a bunch of people what they should pray for they'll run as fast and as far as possible from a man who's clearly unbalanced."

The pastor pulled his smile but it remained in his

eyes. "So you say. Nevertheless I'll do what I can and I'm telling you now that if and when you need help, think of me. Of us. Of people who I guarantee will be praying for you. And help will come."

Zack raked his hands through his hair. "Sure. Anything you say." He was quiet a moment before continuing. "You've been right about everything so far so I won't say you're insane about this. But it feels like you are venturing along the edge of reality."

"Trust me on this." Pastor Johnathon rose, followed by Dennis Penning. Then he turned to me. "And you, Lexi, must be ready to help Zack." My eyes widened. "The two of you connect on a deep emotional level." My face turned red and so did Zack's but neither of us denied the truth of his words. "So you will be the first one Zack thinks about if things get bad. It's how people react in extreme situations. Your emotional connection will enable communication in the heat of battle. And communicating with Lexi will be the first step in bringing help. So it's important, Lexi."

He leaned towards me, placing a hand lightly on my shoulder. "Be ready, Lexi, because the connection between you and Zack may well be the deciding factor in the coming battle."

I stopped breathing. Stopped thinking. I went numb until Zack, seated across from me, reached over and took my hands in his. He didn't say anything and neither did the other men as they turned to leave. But the feel of his hands on mine was enough to break the stasis I was in.

I smiled and that smile came from deep inside of me. Because Pastor Johnathon had given me one thing I could do. I loved Zack and love was what he and

Dennis Penning were talking about. Connecting. Reaching out. Linking souls. So I lifted my shoulders in a casual motion and simply said, "Piece of cake."

Because even though I had no idea how I'd achieve such an impossible feat, if I was needed I'd manage. I'd do it and I'd do it well.

CHAPTER 18

When the pastor and missionary left we headed to town after giving up on whatever work we'd laid out for ourselves for the day. The tension in the air – in the day itself – that no amount of pretending could dispel made work impossible. Finally Zack lay his hammer on that huge table and looked at me where I'd been trying to wrap a cracked lamp base in string that would eventually be glued until it resembled fired clay. "We need to get out of here."

I put the lamp down, relieved to be free of it. "We need a break."

"And we need to talk about something other than demons."

"Plus, we're out of donuts." As good a reason as any to stop working.

We took his truck because we'd possibly go dumpster diving to find something to bring back and upcycle. Just suggesting it was a shout of defiance, a way of telling ourselves we'd be around long enough to do something with whatever we found. To work on it and then take it to the art and craft store to add to their inventory while we gossiped with the owners as it was processed. To be normal. To be alive.

The first place we went was the café where we enjoyed donuts and coffee and carried a rather large bag of a variety of donuts back to the truck for consumption that evening as we watched day turn into night.

Then we wandered over to the Arthur's art and craft store to see if any tourists had found it yet. If so, then the summer season had officially begun.

A dizzy spell came over me as we approached the door. I put out a hand to Zack and his arm came around my waist, supporting me, as it opened and Cameron Blackwell, the artist, came through into the bright day. Though I couldn't smell anything I assumed whatever paint he used in his rather depressing pictures clung to his clothing and had caused the dizziness, same as the other times.

He smiled when he saw us and stopped and greeted us politely. "Summer is almost here, along with tourists who will buy our wares."

"Can't come too soon for me," Zack responded in a voice that was polite but cool as he continued to hold me and subtly back away from Cameron and pointedly waited for him to move aside so we could enter the store.

Cameron stayed put, leaning against the door frame. "I brought a couple more pictures. The Arthurs were happy to have them." He made a motion that could have been preening. "They sell well." He looked at us, clearly empty handed. His eyebrows rose in question. "You?"

"Nothing today," Zack said, tight lipped. "We've been busy with the house." Which meant we had to explain about Zack's fixer-upper and that delayed Cameron's departure and my recovery from whatever was on him that knocked me sidewise every time I got too close.

Zack peered at me. His eyebrows drew together and he considered Cameron. "But it's getting late. I think we'll head back home." And he swept me along with him as he turned around and strode away.

As soon as we were a few yards away, my strength returned and I was soon able to climb into the truck unaided, something I'd not have been able to do if Cameron had been near. "He's weird," I said as Zack slammed his door and started the engine. "And he makes me weird."

"He's not only weird, he's arrogant." He eased the truck onto the road and headed out. The sun poured through the windows, the wind from our passing blew my hair every which way and the scent of early summer flowers permeated everything as Zack continued. "I dislike arrogant people intensely."

I leaned against the back of the seat and enjoyed the passing scenery. It was lovely and I was glad to be alive and sharing this moment with Zack.

I examined him. His hands on the steering wheel, strong and relaxed. How the wind that turned my hair into a mess did nothing to his because he wore his short. How the fabric of his jeans emphasized his thigh muscles and sent a sizzle through my midsection.

Nothing, not even the coming battle, could take away from what was suddenly a special moment because right then, in that truck, life was normal. I was next to a total male stud and knowing I turned him on as much as he turned me on sent me into a happy orbit.

I let my thoughts run riot. As I examined the world beyond the rolled down window I knew that even the meeting with Cameron Blackwell couldn't ruin either the day or the short trip home through sunshine and alongside vacationers enjoying the day.

We didn't work when we got home, though. The trip to town had been a much needed break but wasn't enough to push the coming battle completely from our minds. As one person, we sank into the lounges on my aunt's deck and stared at the glitter of sun on water beyond the tiny beach. Zack spoke almost out of nowhere. "What do you think about what the pastor said?"

"About what?" He'd said a lot.

"You and me connecting. Mentally, I guess, because that's what it sounded like he was suggesting."

"If you need help."

"Exactly." His eyes half closed in thought. "Was it a random remark? Or are we meant to take it literally?"

"You think we can connect mentally?" If so, I could become a conduit for that help the pastor promised.

"Maybe. It's a thought." He turned to me. Those half closed eyes saw everything. All of me. "We already connect emotionally. So would a mental connection be that much harder?"

Our gazes met and held as we both wondered the same thing. "How do we find out?"

"We could call the pastor and ask."

"Or we could try it ourselves."

"How do you propose we start?"

Instead of answering, I closed my eyes. I didn't want to because I loved drowning in those sky blue eyes of his but surely a mental connection would require something different. Something inside of us instead of a look between us.

Once my eyes were closed, I thought what to do next but nothing came to me so I opened them to see what Zack was doing. His eyes, too, were shut. He was trying to connect with me. Mind to mind. Heart to heart. Soul to soul.

I closed my eyes once more and concentrated. What to do? How to connect? Then I knew. I concentrated my entire mind on Zack himself. Zack the man. The things about him that had held me in thrall during our ride home and before, ever since our first meeting when I was locked out of the cottage. His body. How his presence pulled me to him against any resistance on my part. How I sometimes thought we were surely two parts of the same thing.

Then it happened.

It was so total and so unexpected that my eyes flew open. I found myself staring into Zack's eyes because he, too, was feeling it. "We connected."

"It's amazing."

"Can we do it again?"

We shut our eyes and once more I found myself in some alternate universe, searching for Zack, wanting him, needing him. And once more, it happened.

"It's not words."

"It doesn't have to be words."

"Because we don't need words. We just know."

"Intuition?"

"Telepathy?"

"Is it emotional or mental?"

"It doesn't matter. We don't and never will understand and that's okay because it's enough that we can do it."

"We will do it."

"If the battle goes sidewise. If I need help. Which I won't." Typical Zack. The man oozed self-confidence. But I was glad for this new weapon in our arsenal. For every weapon. Because we might need them all.

"You should work on your house."

"No."

"No?"

"Not until after the battle."

"It's your home. You can't just leave it unfinished."

"It's a house. Boards and paint. It can wait. What's coming can't wait and I plan to use every minute – every second – between now and then preparing."

"How?" How did soldiers prepare for battle when they were as ready as possible but had time to pass until the big moment? How to not lose that essential edge?

"It's mental." I could see it in his body, a deliberate thing that started at the top of him and continued to the bottom, as each muscle group went into resting mode. "And emotional. And physical."

"How do you do that? How do you prepare? How do you relax?" Because he did both things, it was easy to see.

He chuckled. "Years of practice. It's what soldiers do when there's nothing to do but wait. Might as well enjoy the day which I hope will include what we just did because connecting mentally was awesome."

He sighed. "It felt good and that feeling, more than any target practice or exercises or strategizing, is what I need right now. Whatever we did a minute or so ago melded me and turned me into something new. Something different. I could feel it."

"A weapon?"

He shrugged. "Maybe. I don't know what it was."

The sun dipped towards the horizon. Night was coming. "I wonder what the demon will say tonight."

Zack examined the horizon that was gathering red streaks and purple shadows. "Guess we'll find out when it comes." He sighed. "And it will come. It always does."

He was right about the demon coming but that night was different from previous visits. It didn't stay long. Didn't whisper much. Didn't boast about its accomplishments or remind us what would happen when it took our souls.

Instead it briefly and unemotionally mentioned the coming battle. "Are you ready, Zack? I don't have to prepare. I'm always ready. But you, mere mortal, should do what you can to fight me."

Zack's reply was nonchalant. "I'm ready."

"Excellent because I love a good fight. You will lose, of course, but I hope you make it interesting before you die."

"Don't worry, Demon. Just show up. I'll be there and if you're not a coward so will you."

Another chuckle in that dark that was blacker than black with frissons of fire and the odor of sulfur. Then the demon abruptly left and normal night sounds returned.

"He didn't stay long."

"Maybe he can't spare the time. Perhaps, in spite of what he said, even demons need to prepare."

"I hope so."

It returned the following night and every night that week. As usual. But it never stayed long or did much.

No theatrics. No sulfur or fire on the walls. Just a brief reminder of what was to come. A battle to determine whether our souls remained intact or whether the demon would lose. But it never sounded concerned.

Then the day came when according to the calendar on the wall one week had passed since Zack and the demon had agreed to fight. It was all I could do to keep down the small amount of the huge breakfast Zack had made that he ate with gusto. But he didn't ask why I was so quiet and ate so little. He knew why.

When we finished eating, he came around to my side of the table and gathered me in his arms as gently as a new-born babe. "It'll be okay, sweetheart. I'll win. I promise. And I always keep my promises."

I whimpered uncontrollably and pressed myself close, as hard as possible, feeling his body, his warmth, and taking in the scent of wood shavings and man and that indefinable something that made him who and what he was as he whispered into my hair. "I'll finish my house and we'll live there together for many wonderful years. And that's another promise."

CHAPTER 19

The day passed quietly. The pastor and Dennis Penning showed up around noon, quiet and solemn. They didn't say much when they arrived but, over the course of the afternoon, a few things came clear. Mostly from pastor Johnathon.

"That army I spoke of." Zack looked around with a small smile at the empty beach and the thicket between our places that held birds and small animals but no soldiers. No weapons. No people at all. "That army is in place. That is, it will be in place this evening. I'll stay with them so I won't be here. But Dennis will be."

Zack's eyebrows rose and the pastor answered his unspoken question. "The congregation. Not all of them, of course, but enough."

"They are the army? In a church?" Zack blinked. "You have civilians standing around in church and you tell me they are an army?"

The pastor smiled. "It is indeed an army. As promised. A prayer army." At Zack's raised eyebrows, he added, "Don't discount prayer. It's powerful."

Then the pastor looked at me. "And Lexi, here, she'll be the conduit if you call for help." Then he added, seemingly at random. "Remember, Zack, this will be a fight between good and evil. The demon is evil. You are a good man but you are only a man. One man. That should be enough but it never hurts to have additional weapons on call."

Zack didn't respond but I saw their looks connect. The pastor's gaze was calm. Almost peaceful. Zack's eyes were tiger eyes. Warrior eyes.

Then the sun touched the tops of the trees. They were tall trees so it wasn't dusk yet but time was passing and soon it would begin. The battle that would decide my fate and Zack's.

It could have been my imagination but I swore I felt a sudden change. A chill in the air, followed almost immediately by the heat of unseen fire. And the smell of sulfur. No, it wasn't imaginary. It was real.

"It's here." My words were soft but everyone heard. "The demon is here."

The pastor nodded. "I'll leave now. I wish you luck. Not that you need it. You're awesome, Zack. You'll win." He turned to go. "But know that army is in place."

Zack didn't hear. He'd felt the change in the air and knew what it meant and he was already someplace unknown, wherever warriors go as a battle begins. A place I didn't know and never would and where I couldn't follow no matter how I wished to be there with him.

A darkness spread across the landscape. Not the dark of dusk or night, rather it was the dark of the demon's visits. I turned towards that eerie darkness, afraid of what was there but needing to see the enemy. To look it in the eye. The demon that had been tormenting me.

A figure strode towards us, darker than the darkness if such was possible. A man, or so it seemed, clad all in black and holding what appeared to be a sword. He – or 'it' because what Zack was about to fight couldn't possibly be human so must be a demon in human form. It came closer, enough to make out its features.

I gasped. "Cameron Blackwell."

"The artist that made you sick. The evil in Lewsitown." Zack spoke in a low voice as suddenly, without anything happening that I could see, a pure white sword, shining and bright and filling the space around it with luminous light appeared in his hand and I remembered what the pastor had said. Beside me, Dennis Penning murmured. "The sword of the spirit."

Just as suddenly, without me seeing how it happened, Zack was clad in shining armor. A knight of old. Dennis Penning continued to murmur. "The belt of truth. The breastplate of righteousness, the shoes of peace and the helmet of salvation. All to match the sword of the spirit." He smiled. "He is armed."

This would be a battle between good and evil, between the forces of light and dark and I now saw that it would be fought with black and white swords in this small space between our homes against the backdrop of the tiny forest where birds and small animals lived.

Except there was no sign of life in that forest now. It had gone silent. Completely. The animals that lived there must have somehow known what was about to happen because every living thing that could leave had done so.

Dennis Penning lay a hand on Zack's shoulder. "You can do this, Zack. I know you can."

Zack grinned briefly as Cameron Blackwell approached close and then closer still. Zack the warrior was still there but the whole of him was somehow transformed. Changed. He was now the cheerful singer of off-key songs I'd fallen in love with and also a battle-tested warrior ready to eliminate pure evil. But there was also some other Zack. A shining knight I'd not been able to imagine if he wasn't standing before me. And the new combined Zack was confident and unafraid.

He turned away from Dennis Penning and me. He and Cameron Blackwell strode towards each other. Eagerness was evident in each of them. They wanted this. Each wanted to do battle and each expected to win. They raised their swords in salute until they were pointed at the heavens.

Then, in sync, the swords came down and arced through the air towards each other, dark fire and white light trailing their movements. And as quickly as that, the battle began.

Swords clashed. I remembered physical ed fencing classes from when I was a kid so I recognized the studied, precise, back and forth movements. It was a dance during which they were testing each other, feeling out their opponent, studying how and what they did. It was how duels were fought. I knew that.

Then the fight changed. Instead of the studied, delicate parries and thrusts of fencing the fight turned ugly. Brutal. They slashed and struck at each other, all pretense of civility gone, seeking to end the fight quickly and completely. To slash their opponent into bloody, torn chunks and pieces. To destroy them.

But it didn't happen. Both were equally adept,

equally agile, dark fire and bright light mingling and swirling and flashing in every direction. Their swords ground against each other as they sought to overcome the other through sheer physical strength until the sound of metal against metal screamed through the air to where Dennis Penning and I stood watching in thrall, unable to do anything. Unable to help.

It felt like it lasted forever. Thrust and parry. Chop and stab. One handed with precision, two handed with brutal force. Nothing made a difference. Not *the* difference. They were too well matched. So it became a battle of endurance, a matter of which would lose their edge first. When that happened, when one of them grew weary and let up their guard the least bit, the other would go in for the kill.

The battlefield grew until it encompassed the entirety of the small forest between our houses. Trees fell, slashed by their swords. Leaves curled into nothingness and moonlight shone through the spaces where those trees had stood. And silence grew except for the sound of metal against metal as their swords met.

The demon – Cameron Blackwell or whatever evil thing was occupying his body – paused minutely and spread his legs, screaming in a language I'd never heard. A guttural, visceral language. Asking for help. For strength. And it came, in the form of even greater darkness surging up from the ground, with fire licking a path to the demon.

As the fire reached it, the demon screamed again, raised its sword, and ran straight at Zack. I screamed too. No way could Zack or any human withstand this new threat. He'd lose.

But Zack called on reserves I'd not thought he had and held his sword in front of him like a protective barrier and the attack stopped. Momentarily. But Zack was weakening. He couldn't keep it up forever. All the demon had to do was keep the pressure on Zack until he could no longer protect himself and the demon was strong with the help that had come from Hell.

The end was in sight. Dennis Penning turned to me. "Now! Do it now!"

"What?" I looked at him in confusion. Then I knew and I closed my eyes, hard as it was to look away from Zack when he was in such danger, and threw my mind towards him. Gave him myself. What strength I had.

It helped. When I opened my eyes, he'd straightened a bit. But it wasn't enough.

"We need that army," Dennis Penning said. "Do it again but this time call for the pastor. For help."

I didn't know if I could do it. Zack and I had practiced communicating silently but I'd not tried with anyone else. But Zack was dying. I had to do something. So, terrified that I'd screw up, that I'd do it wrong, that I'd not connect with the pastor, I closed my eyes again. Whimpered in sheer terror. And thought of the pastor.

Suddenly, without warning, a white beam arced through the sky, flashing and sparking and strong and true. It came from the direction of town – from the church where the pastor and congregation were praying – and went straight towards Zack. Into him, then through him and into his sword where it crackled and shone and blazed with renewed light. And Zack, energized and strong once more, raised that sword now flashing with a brilliance beyond believing, and threw it at the demon.

His aim was true. The sword pierced the demon's heart. If it had a heart. And just like that, the battle was over and the demon disappeared in a cloud of smoke and fire and sulfur and screams such as I'd never heard before and never wanted to hear again. A cloud rose high above the trees, billowing black smoke with flames shooting everywhere as those screams grew louder and worse with the fire growing and growing. Until, as suddenly as if a door was shut, the earth swallowed everything and it all ended. Disappeared. Nothing remained. Nothing at all.

Zack stood, stunned, and looked around. Looked for the demon – for Cameron Blackwell – and found nothing. Just the forest as it had been before the battle began, the trees restored and the grass beneath our feet green and growing and as normal as grass could be. He looked up, into the sky, but all he saw – all any of us saw – were stars and a crescent moon and wisps of clouds visible in the night sky, backlit by a sun that had set but still managed to shine minimally on the highest clouds.

He turned all the way around. Twice. He was unable to take in that it was over. That the demon was gone forever. Dennis Penning and I did the same, watching from the sidelines as we'd done during the battle. Unable to move. To think. To do anything except gaze upon the night and the man still standing while remembering what had just happened. A battle we'd never have believed if we hadn't seen it ourselves and would never be able to tell anyone about because they'd never believe us.

Time passed agonizingly slow. Reality returned.

Zack looked at his empty hand, the sword gone, as if wondering whether it had ever been there at all. And shook his shoulders to remind himself that he was no longer clothed in armor.

I regained the ability to move. I went to him, took the hand in mine that had so recently held a sword of light and power that had sent an evil being into nothingness. I spoke. "You did it, Zack. You won."

He blinked. "Piece of cake." He gathered himself and returned to the world we knew. "But I had help. I couldn't have done it without help. Without the prayers I didn't think I needed."

"The demon had help. Of course you needed help too."

He thought about that. He nodded. Then he blinked again. "You're free, Lexi. Free. We are both free." And we just stood there, both of our hands clasped though neither knew how we'd gone from me holding just one hand to both of us holding hands like a couple of teenagers. We let the reality of what had just happened sink into us as he managed to speak once more. "We are free once more to live our lives."

I smiled. "You can finish your house."

"And you can make all kinds of awesome stuff."

He smiled but it was an awkward smile and he struggled to get it right. Though I knew, because I knew him, that he'd spent more of his life smiling than frowning, that the battle had taken away that inborn ability. He had to think how to move his lips. To puzzle out how to make them turn up at the corners. But he figured it out. He managed. "But about the house, Lexi, it's not my house. It's our house and we'll live there together."

He drew me close and we came together gently, carefully, afraid that if we were too happy something would go wrong and the demon would resurrect and we'd not live the life we'd just been given. But we managed.

Zack reached normalcy first, pushing away our fears and lifting my chin until we were eye to eye. "We'll do it, Lexi, we'll be happy and I'll work on the house and we'll move in as soon as we get married."

He paused, thinking, as Zack the warrior left in tiny increments and Zack the builder returned full-on. "I can have it livable in a few days if I work hard. That'll mean we can live there immediately even if we get married as soon as we can get a license and arrangements can be made." His eyes quirked a question at me. "Which is what I'd like. If you agree to marry me, that is, and I think you will."

I broke eye contact and leaned into his shirt and murmured into it, my words muffled but clear enough. "Sounds good to me. Let's do it." Then I added, "ASAP."

CHAPTER 20

We were married in the church in town. Of course we were, no place else would do, with pastor Johnathon presiding and my entire family in attendance even though some of them had to change their plans to be there on such short notice. My aunt Gertrude paid a fortune for a quick flight from Europe and insisted it was worth it.

Most of the attendees drove and camped at the local campground because all the motels were full. Tourist season was in full swing but, as my uncle commented, a few days extra after the wedding meant they could both attend a wedding and enjoy a vacation afterwards.

Zack's parents, the only family he had, camped next to my parents and they all sat around the same campfire and made s'mores together. My mother insisted it was a bonding experience.

The church was full even though there weren't enough family members to fill it because the pastor sneakily invited the entire congregation. He told them it would be a way for them to get to know us, the new members.

Privately he said it was his way of thanking the

prayer army for saving our lives and our souls. "They'll have a nice meal. Payment for services rendered." As he told us that, he reached for a second piece of the wedding cake that had been baked by a member of the congregation, a woman who'd stayed up that night and prayed as hard as she knew how though she knew not what she was praying for.

"I told them some of it," Pastor Johnathon said as he finished that second slice of cake with a sigh of contentment. "They saw the fire in the sky and they knew it appeared right after their prayers were needed. They'd felt the need. They'd felt their prayers being used. Then they saw the fire. It was brief but it lit up the whole sky." His eyes slit in remembrance. "They asked about it and I told them what they saw was evil being defeated. They were curious but they didn't ask questions. They merely said they were glad to help."

Aunt Gertrude decided to stay in her cottage for the remainder of the summer instead of returning to Europe. "Europe has nothing I don't already have right here. A lovely lake, friendly people, a nearby town with everything a tourist could wish for, including donuts to die for and trinkets for everyone from that nice store next to the donuts." She, too, sighed in contentment as she asked how Zack and I had managed to become friends after our contentious meeting when he thought I was breaking into her cottage.

I took a second piece of wedding cake for myself. It was very good and I love cake almost as much as donuts. "It was his singing while working on his house that did it. That attracted me. The music. The songs. I didn't know it was him, of course, but I liked the sound of it."

Aunt Gertrude harrummped. "Didn't happen. That tiny forest between the two places is much too thick for any sound to penetrate. Believe me I know. I yelled myself hoarse when you were a kid and visited and wanted to explore that dangerous wreck of a house next door. You never heard and I screamed. Loudly." Her eyebrows rose in a cheeky fashion. "I guarantee you didn't hear Zack singing because it was impossible, which means it was love that brought you two together. Pure love. It overcame the sound barrier." She sighed in ecstasy. "Isn't love grand?"

I didn't argue but knew what I'd heard and that I'd heard Zack singing before I knew who he was. Which meant I'd heard those songs for a different reason. Because I needed to hear them. Because the singer would save my life. And my soul. As I thought those thoughts I realized I'd never actually know if that was the reason. But it didn't matter because whatever the reason was, I'd forever be glad it happened the way it did.

As we left the church and started our lives as a married couple, we acknowledged that we had one more thing to do before we could settle into a routine of an old married couple. We'd bring more of my creations to the Arthur's store as soon as possible because, what with taking everything of mine out of the cottage and dumping them in our new home, things were crowded because there were already boards everywhere and tools and my junk just added to the clutter The more things we could get out of the house and in a store, the fewer we'd have to deal with and the more income potential we'd have.

So the next morning, on our first full day as a

married couple, we loaded the pickup and went to town. Ross and Delia Arthur were happy to take everything we brought. We were surprised. Delia's eyebrows rose as Arthur explained. "We have more space than expected." His voice was wry. "Since that no-good artist took off on us."

"Who do you mean?" Even as I politely asked, I knew who they meant.

"Cameron Blackwell, that's who." Arthur couldn't keep the irritation out of his words. "Took every single picture of his out of the store. Didn't tell us he was doing it. Didn't ask." He raked the back of his neck in frustration. "Don't know how he did it, either. We just came to work one morning and his pictures were gone. Every single one. But the store was still locked and there was no evidence of a break-in. Nothing."

Delia took up the story. "We couldn't imagine what had happened. We called the police, thinking there'd been a break-in. They went to Cameron's house to see what they could find out. But he was gone. Lock, stock, and barrel. All his pictures, everything he owned. All of it. All gone."

Arthur finished the story. "The police were soon inundated by people who had bought Cameron's pictures. Paid a lot of money for them. Had them hanging in their homes. And, just as with the pictures in our store, their pictures disappeared overnight. Gone. Just gone. And those poor people were out all that money."

Delia shuddered. "At least the pictures in our store were on commission so we didn't lose any money. But I pity the people who did."

Zack said mildly, "They were awful pictures. The

world is better off without them."

I couldn't help adding, "The world is better off without Cameron Blackwell."

Arthur thought about what we'd said. "Yes. You are right. But there was something about those pictures. They were strangely appealing to some people." He shuddered and it was clear Cameron's pictures didn't appeal to him. Of course they didn't. Arthur was a nice person.

With the pickup empty, we grabbed a sack full of donuts from the café next door and returned to the house we now lived in that was unfinished but done enough that we could make do. No inside walls except for the bathroom and the kitchen was a skeleton of what it would become but it functioned. We had water and electricity and heat and air conditioning. All the essentials.

We should have gotten right to work when we reached home. Put up a wall. Cut some sheet-rock. Measured for trim. Something. Instead we sat on the couch that was our first joint purchase for our new home that we'd placed where we could sit and look through those huge picture windows over a lake that gleamed and sparkled in the bright sunshine. As brightly as the sword of the spirit that Zack had wielded so effectively.

We sat there all that day, mostly silent, occasionally saying something or another. Nothing important. The important thing was being there. Together. Happy. Alive. With our souls intact.

That night we retired to the mattress on the floor that passed for our bed in what would someday be a bedroom. After making love we curled into each other and slept the night through. Nothing woke us up. No demons. Nothing.

In the morning, Zack would awaken first. As usual. And he'd make breakfast, singing loudly and totally off-key and I'd pretend to still sleep so I could enjoy the racket as I happily looked forward to a lifetime of equally amazing, wonderful musical mornings.

THE END

Hi,

I hope you enjoyed *Soul Wars – Lexi*.

If you'd like to leave a review, click on the link beneath the *Soul Wars – Lexi* cover on my authors website – http://www.FlorenceWitkop.com – and you'll find yourself on the Amazon page where you can let people know what you think. Though reviews aren't absolutely essential for sales, I enjoy hearing from my readers and seeing my books through their eyes.

If you want to see other books I've written, just check out my website – and here's the link (again): http://www.FlorenceWitkop.com

Now for the new stuff:

My next book is *Spaceship Mercy*. It's a contemporary, clean and wholesome romance with a healthy dose of science fiction. I must admit that I write the kind of clean romances I love to read about normal, well-adjusted, everyday people who unexpectedly find themselves in abnormal situations. Of course, I often also include a generous helping of science fiction and/or paranormal elements. And action. And adventure.

Here's the back cover info that tells what *Spaceship Mercy* is about:

She wanted to travel. She didn't expect a spaceship.

Chloe's new neighbor, ripped ex-soldier Mac, is as interested in her as she is in him and they both enjoy counting shooting stars on warm summer nights.

But one shooting star isn't a natural phenomenon. It's a spaceship with a badly injured alien inside who's on a galactic mission of mercy.

Former military pilot Mac agrees to help complete the mission. He tells Chloe she can't come. He doesn't tell her why.

But Chloe has seldom traveled so on impulse she stows away, unaware she was left behind because the trip will be extremely dangerous. Bloodthirsty pirates are after the cargo of priceless medicine necessary to end a deadly plague.

The pirates find the spaceship. They board it. Capture Chloe. Hold her hostage. And force Mac to choose: save the woman he loves or the entire population of a distant planet.

SPACESHIP *MERCY*

by

Florence Witkop

CHAPTER 1

I'm a small-town girl. Never traveled except to college and that was in the same state. The man beside me, however, had traveled extensively during his years as a military pilot. He'd been everywhere.

But he chose my hometown when he left the service and as we sat and watched the day slowly disappear, I was content to be on his balcony. Nowhere else. We weren't officially a couple but I was pretty sure I wasn't the only one thinking it was just a matter of time.

At that moment, though, all that mattered was that I was totally content and I sighed mightily as I let my eyes rove over the solid male form beside me.

"Nice, huh?" He gestured to the scene spreading before us, thinking my love of western landscapes was behind my sigh, not knowing he himself was the cause. He considered the scenery further and nodded to himself, agreeing with what he thought my sigh had meant. That the scenery was lovely. "Gaunt. Lots of land and most of it's barren. But I like it."

"Me too. Gorgeous." No reason for him to know

I'd been admiring him instead of the scenery. We went quiet then, just taking in the vista. Miles of western countryside without buildings or power lines or much of anything beyond sky, brown scrub bushes and a few trees.

Mac pointed to the sky, still blue but growing darker as evening approached with the western horizon just starting to turn its riotous evening shades of pink and red and violet. "I never get tired of watching the sun set."

With which he wrapped an arm around me and pulled me close and we stayed that way while those pinks darkened to violet and the landscape beneath the sunset turned a medium shade of purple and then darker as we watched.

Then suddenly, with no warning at all, a ball of fire streaked across the purple sky and disappeared in one of the many small valleys that dotted the landscape. A plume of fire erupted and burned high and hot where it had disappeared but was gone as quickly as it came. The whole thing happened so fast, barely more than a second, that if we hadn't been watching that exact piece of sky at that exact moment, we'd have missed it entirely.

Mac's arm left my shoulders as we both sat up straight and stared. "Meteor?"

"A meteor that size would have caused an earthquake." The ground hadn't moved.

"Plane?"

"If it was a plane, it crashed. And burned."

"The fire didn't last long."

"So it didn't burn up completely."

"Which means there could be survivors."

"Who need help."

"Cutters Gap is too small for emergency response services."

"Then it's up to us."

"There are a million valleys in that direction. Can we even find it?"

Mac looked towards where the fireball had disappeared. "I think I know the place. There are two large dead trees on the edge of a valley. They are all gnarly and twisted so it's easy to differentiate that valley from others. It's where I hunt. Whatever just went down is either in that valley or nearby. It's the only valley with those two specific trees."

"So that's where we start to look?" He nodded. "Are there roads?"

He shook his head. "None but we'll take my truck. The crash site is pretty far off the road if I saw it right. The terrain is rough. But my truck can handle it." His old, battered but well-cared-for four-wheel-drive pickup.

His apartment was on the second floor. We were down the stairs and in his truck as fast as we could move and Mac peeled onto the road on two wheels and then flew through the two streets of our small town as if pursued by the devil.

When he reached open territory, he went even faster and I prayed we'd survive. But he seemed to know what he was doing. Had he been a race car driver in a previous life?

It took longer than expected to reach the small valley with the two dead trees because the country distance was deceptive and we crossed more miles than I'd thought possible before he slowed as we reached the beginning of the valley with those two dead trees and began a slow, careful descent to the bottom, avoiding boulders and following game trails wherever possible until we reached the bottom. And saw what had come from the sky with fire trailing behind.

My breath stopped. "It can't be."

"It's impossible."

"Except it's there."

"It's real."

At the bottom of the valley, at the end of a deep trench it had plowed through the earth and trees and rocks, lay a spaceship.

A spaceship!

Dents along one side spoke of the rough ride through the dirt and a darkened hull spoke of the fire that had tried to burn it up as it blazed through the sky. It was huge, larger than a very large jet but round which meant it had more space inside than even the largest commercial plane.

"Whoever the pilot is, he's good." Mac, the pilot, spoke to himself. "He kept it under control and kept the ship intact. Amazing." He shut off the truck and jumped to the ground and sprinted towards the spaceship. I followed, stumbling over rocks and avoiding prickly bushes.

A door appeared on the side of the spaceship. One second the surface was smooth except for the dents of its rough landing, the next there was an opening. We waited with bated breath for someone – or something – to come out.

Nothing happened. "He's hurt," was Mac's cryptic statement. "He opened the door automatically, hoping someone would come and help."

"How do you know that?"

"I don't. I'm guessing. But if I'm right, there's someone in that weird craft who needs our help." He slanted a look at me. "I'm going in." Then he added, "Don't follow me." He nailed me with that look. "In case I'm wrong I want you safe."

"I'm coming. You can't stop me."

He sighed knowing I'd not obey him, then shook his head and gestured. "Stay behind me. If I tell you to get out, you do so immediately. Understood?" He shoved his face in mine, brows furrowed.

"Yes." It was all I could manage, all there was time for even if I'd had a better response because as we talked we'd been moving and were now beside the spaceship. He examined the door and peered inside.

"I don't see anyone." He strode up the ramp that had magically appeared along with the door. He turned back to me, that frown still in place. "Remember what I said! Don't assume anything. Don't be brave. Run as fast as possible if anything – anything at all – makes you uncomfortable. Or if I tell you to."

I nodded and followed him inside. There was light from some unknown source and the sound of metal groaning from where the crash had damaged the ship. Then we faintly heard another sound. A soft moaning. "Someone is alive."

Mac followed the moans along some kind of corridor. When we turned a corner into what was probably the control room of the ship, we saw a single being. Not a person. A being. It was strapped in a chair but the straps were all that kept it from falling to the floor because it was hurt.

It was humanoid and sort of like all the depictions

of little green men because it definitely was green and smaller than me and I'm barely five two. Thin arms and legs were at odd angles that would mean broken bones in a human.

It looked at us with huge eyes. Blinked. Asked silently for help. Mac responded by clicking loose the straps that held it in place and easing it to the floor where it continued to moan in pain as Mac bent close to its head. "What can we do for you? How can we help?"

The being blinked again. It didn't understand. Mac swore in frustration, bit his lower lip and looked at me. "Now what?"

The being didn't speak, just moaned louder and rocked in pain. Mac was clearly frustrated. "It's an alien. I don't know how to help it."

The being gestured for Mac to move closer. He did and the being touched his forehead. I was sure it was trying to communicate telepathically. I'd seen a documentary once in which believers in little green men said they communicated that way. Now the documentary didn't seem so ridiculous.

But nothing happened. The being just touched Mac's forehead. Then it let its hand drop. Its look of pure frustration was evident. That and hopelessness. And fear because it couldn't tell us how to help it.

Mac shook his head. "So what now?"

We stared at each other, an alien being and Mac and me, all three of us wondering how to communicate.

Then the alien touched its ear. What passed for an ear. It gestured for us to look closer. When we did we saw a tiny device above its ear that was probably implanted. It gestured again, pain almost rendering its meaning unclear. But I understood.

"It's a universal translator."

Mac looked at me. "How do you know that?"

I almost smiled. Almost. "I watch Star Trek."

The alien gestured again, obviously hurting but determined to communicate. It pointed to the panel near its chair. Actually to the cabinet beneath the panel. It gestured again, its eyes staring into ours.

"Look in the cabinet."

I did. The cabinet consisted of drawers, each of which was divided into compartments. Each compartment contained something. I stared. Looked from the contents of that drawer to the device behind the alien's ear. And reached for a similar device.

The alien smiled. If its expression was a smile. I wasn't sure but the situation was too dire to stop and consider subtleties. It was hurt badly.

I took a chance and put the device on the skin just above my ear. And prayed I wasn't killing myself instead of helping the alien. Immediately, I felt a slight shiver and heard a buzz. Then nothing.

The alien watched. Waited. Tipped its head and waited some more. Then, seemingly hearing something in its own ear, it spoke.

"Can you help me?"

I turned to Mac. "It worked. We're talking. He's hurt." 'It' didn't sound right any more. The alien wasn't a thing. It was a living being and I just hoped it was a 'him.' It seemed like a 'him.'

Mac found a second universal translator in another compartment in the drawer and slapped it behind his ear. He went through that same several seconds of not knowing what was happening. Then his face cleared and he simply looked at the alien.

The alien spoke. "There's a medical bay. I'm too badly injured to get there by myself and communication between the medical bay and the bridge was destroyed by the crash landing. If you'd be so kind as to go to the medical bay and bring the medical robot back here, it'll take over."

"It'll heal you?"

"I don't know." The alien kind of looked down at its body. "My injuries are extensive and it's just a robot. A very smart machine. But it'll assess my injuries and fix them if they are fixable."

Mac leaned closer. "Where's this medical bay located?"

It was clear the alien saw hope now that we could communicate. He closed his eyes as he strained to do something. To think. Then a map of the ship appeared in my mind and, I was sure, in Mac's.

The alien spoke to Mac and Mac now nodded. I hadn't heard anything but Mac had and I was happy to let the two of them communicate. Did the alien see that Mac was a take-charge kind of guy? Probably. Mac had the vibe of a leader. Someone who does things instead of watching others. "He said the robot knows how to transport him to the medical bay once we make it understand what's needed and bring it here."

"How do we talk to a robot?"

"I don't know." He looked at me blankly. "Guess we'll find out."

Following Mac, I understood how hard it must have been for people to find their way around the Pentagon until corridors were marked. The craft was round and the corridors were a confusing maze of sameness multiplied many times. But with the help of that mental map we got to the medical bay. Stared at the mechanical thing in the middle of the room that had to be the robot. A large, black box. Approached it. And wondered what to do next.

CHAPTER 2

It proved not to be a problem. The machine – for that's what it was – turned itself on as we grew close and turned towards us. Whirred and clanked a bit. Shone a light on us, then turned the light off and whirred and clanked enough more to and made us wonder if we should run for our lives. And spoke. "Why are you here?" In perfect English.

We looked at one another. "You speak English?"

"Of course." Was its tone condescending? I thought it was, a bit. Like an English butler.

Mac didn't waste time. "We need your help."

"You don't appear to be in any physical distress."

"It's not for us."

It waited patiently as Mac thought what to say next. I beat him to it. "Someone is injured in the control room."

It thought a second or did whatever it did that substituted for thought. "Are you referring to the bridge?"

Mac was military. He knew what that meant. "Yes. The bridge. Something – someone – on the bridge is injured and asked us to come to you for help."

"Why didn't you bring him here?"

"We were afraid we'd make his injuries worse."

The machine whirred more. "I'll go now." And wheels we'd not noticed until then rolled it smoothly through the door and back the way we'd come.

"It didn't bring a stretcher." We half ran to catch up with the machine.

"Maybe it doesn't need one."

Soon the three of us, two humans and a robot, crowded through the door to what I now knew was the bridge. The machine was beside the injured being before we were through, lowering itself to the floor where the alien lay in obvious pain that seemed to grow worse with each passing minute.

Mac's hand stopped me from going close. "We shouldn't interfere."

The robot, the black boxy thing, settled completely to the floor, its wheels retracting. A thin sheet of something solid slid out from its bottom and carefully, gently, slid under the alien and wrapped around him until the small, green being was fully enclosed. Then the robot rose back to its normal height, bringing the alien up with it. Then it turned just as gently and left the bridge.

We followed as it moved through the maze of corridors back to the medical bay we'd just left but it did so much slower than it had rolled to the bridge. Because it was carrying an injured being and shouldn't make the injuries worse.

It didn't prevent us from following. Again, we watched from across the room as what might have been an operating table slid out of the wall and a myriad of instruments appeared seemingly from nowhere. Lights flashed. A bright beam ran the length of the alien.

"It's checking for what's wrong."

It also, apparently, put the alien to sleep because, as we watched, the pain disappeared from its eyes. *His* eyes. I reminded myself the alien wasn't an '*it*.' Then those huge eyes closed and *he* seemed to relax completely as the instruments moved closer, cutting off clothes and probing flesh. If that's what the alien was encased in. Probably it was flesh. All done with the medical robot overseeing everything.

"I guess the robot is in charge. It's hovering over the alien and I suspect it's telling the machines what to do." Even though we couldn't hear anything. Electronic communication?

The robot heard. Turned to us. And spoke. "You are correct. I am supervising the healing of the Captain."

Mac asked the only important question. "Can he be fixed?" Mac called the alien '*he*.' I was humbled and a bit embarrassed that I'd had to figure it out while Mac just knew no being of any kind is an '*it*.'

"Of course." After a pause, it added, "Though whether his injuries can be repaired to pre-accident status, I can't say. They are extensive." The robot called the Captain 'him.' Earth wasn't the only place with two sexes. Good to know.

How long will it take?"

The robot seemed to think. "Healing varies with each species and each individual so there's no precise way to determine the amount of time required. But several of your Earth days are most likely. One week, perhaps, though if the Captain is in good health – as are all personnel of starships – an entire week will likely bring the Captain to a level at which the final degree of recovery can be determined."

Mac sucked in his breath. "We'll have to keep people away from this valley for a week at least. Maybe more if he can't fly the ship and leave by then." He turned to me. "You're local. I just moved here. Is that possible?"

I thought a moment. "Probably. As far as I know no one saw the ship come down except us. I didn't see any other vehicles coming this way and if anyone had seen it they'd be here now with bells on along with everyone else in a hundred mile radius because local gossip is insanely efficient. Five minutes, tops."

"What about someone finding it accidentally?"

"This valley is off the beaten path and it isn't hunting season. So we're probably okay in that regard for now. But if the ship is damaged beyond repair, it'll be found eventually."

Mac thought out loud. "It'll also be found if the repairs take a long time." He turned to the robot. "When can we talk with the Captain and find out more?"

"Tomorrow by your time. The repairs to his body will take an hour or so Earth time but then he'll need rest. Much rest. Rest is restorative. But by tomorrow morning, Earth time, he should be functional enough to communicate rationally."

"So we come back tomorrow morning."

I looked around at the room we were in and remembered the many corridors and the bridge. The spaceship was huge. Lots of rooms. "Why not stay here tonight?"

Mac rubbed the back of his neck. "Because we don't know what alien beings in weird spaceships do in this or any other situation. How they live and eat and so on. If their food would poison us. Things we must know if we stay overnight. Most of all, we don't know if they allow humans to stay overnight and what might happen if they don't. And since the Captain isn't functional, we can't ask."

I looked around again. "It's a spaceship! Aren't

you curious?"

"Insanely so but I'm also prudent. It's not just the Captain. It's the ship itself. Who knows what space ships do. Maybe it'll function autonomously when it figures out the Captain is injured and will simply decide to return to space. With us on board."

He had a point. I didn't want to end up halfway across the galaxy because I slept through an automatic take-off. Mac turned back to the robot. "What can you tell me about the ship? Is it reparable? Is it autonomous?"

"I cannot answer those questions. Mechanics are beyond my expertise."

"Who does know?"

"The Captain." Who was asleep on an operating table surrounded by a tangle of mechanical doctors. "The mechanics also know but they are busy. They are checking and repairing the damage."

"Mechanics?"

"Robots. What you call black boxes. Like me." How'd it know what we called it? "The only living being on this ship is the Captain."

Mac started for the door. "Then we'll leave. We're not staying overnight but we'll be back tomorrow morning. Hopefully no one saw us come and if we leave now no one will have missed us so they won't have a reason to come looking for us."

"We went for a ride." I thought about that. "An all day picnic."

Mac was thinking ahead to the next day. "Perhaps the damage is minimal for a spaceship and it'll be gone when we return. If it's autonomous, that is, which it might be because the Captain must sleep sometime."

Unless little green men didn't need sleep.

I didn't say that out loud. "It would be best if it's gone. Problem solved."

Mac's expression said he hoped the spaceship would still be there. All the time we'd been in it his eyes had flitted everywhere, taking in everything, even while attending to the alien or deciding what to do next. He was a pilot. He'd once said he could fly anything with wings plus a few things that didn't have them.

For any pilot this ship must be the ultimate dream. Of course it was. It came from beyond Earth. Possibly from beyond the solar system. The rush of just being near it must be addicting and looking at him I knew Mac was hooked. He couldn't hide how he felt if he tried. And he didn't try. He simply examined the ship as if he was in a candy store and the ship was chocolate.

We returned to Cutters Gap and the everyday life of a very small town though we were both too keyed up to sleep. We ended up once more on his balcony and we stayed there far into the night, sitting again on chairs with our feet on the railing while sipping cans of pop, though this time with the addition of thick sandwiches that were dinner because cooking was too much work. Finding a damaged spaceship and saving an alien's life had exhausted us emotionally if not physically.

As I finally headed for my apartment I heard Mac's mutter. "Aliens. Space ships. What next?"

I let the door to my place close behind me and wished it could stay open because I didn't want to take a chance on being asleep when Mac woke the next morning. I didn't want to chance him leaving without me and suspected he might do just that. He'd think he'd be keeping me safe while experiencing the thrill of space for himself. No way that was happening. I was coming too.

So I planned a sleepless night watching moonlight march across the bedroom wall but I must have fallen asleep in spite of my intentions because I awoke the next morning actually rested. I quickly downed a cold hot dog because protein is good preparation for a busy day and headed downstairs to find Mac already there and waiting. At least he waited instead of going off by himself. I was grateful.

Mac's truck had been parked behind the apartment building so no one saw us leave and no one was up and about that early anyway. The sun was barely peeking over the horizon and it was midsummer which meant most people were still asleep.

He drove quietly until we were out of town. Then he opened it up and we roared across the scrub ground to the spaceship that was still there, exactly as we'd found it. Mac's wide grin was the only indication that he was glad to see it hadn't taken off and left him without a chance to learn more about it.

The alien was awake and alert enough to communicate. He spoke. "I suggest you implant a communication device permanently in each of you so as to eliminate any possibility of our talks being compromised." He struggled to sit up. "But that's up to you. It's against galactic law to change or add to a being's natural body without their permission."

Mac couldn't wait for the new thing to be done. I wasn't eager to have a foreign device in my body permanently but I didn't say so as Mac asked, "What do we have to do to get the implants? Is there something to sign?"

"You just must agree. The protocol will sense that agreement and proceed accordingly."

The robot – the medical bay black box -- reached out and touched us. Just touched us. Then its hands – or what functioned as hands -- retracted and it said, "It's done."

I was unnerved at the thought that something had been done to me so quickly. The temporary translators had been made permanent in less than a second. What else could it do without me knowing? "You may feel something momentarily. Or not. Species vary as to their sensitivity to bodily alterations."

I tuned in to my body and, yes, there was a faint thrumming I'd not have noticed if the robot hadn't spoken. Mac, too, was experiencing the same thing judging by his expression though he was eager to get on with things and explore this new ability. And the strange craft we were in.

He turned to the alien on the hospital bed, still resting and still weak. "Now we can get somewhere. Figure out what to do next. How to help." He paused. "If you still believe you need help, that is." He examined the alien, still supine on what we were pretty sure had been an operating table and was now a place to rest and heal.

The alien stared at the ceiling the way people do when there's a lot to say but they aren't sure how to begin. "The circumstances of my unfortunate arrival on your planet are concerning."

After a moment's thought, he continued. "I'm glad you found me." His eyes met ours. "Others who have crashed on your planet haven't been so fortunate. They've been imprisoned and their crafts impounded."

"We've no desire to hurt you and will do what we can to help."

"Stopping on Earth wasn't on my itinerary." There was no way to read the alien's feelings, if he had feelings. "Nor was it an accident."

Silence followed that statement until Mac spoke again in a very quiet voice. "Are you saying you were attacked?"

"I'm afraid so."

"Who attacked you? And why?"

The alien sighed so sighs must be a universal emotional reaction. "My cargo is extremely valuable. Worth a lot on the black market." After a moment, he added, "Pirates attacked me."

CHAPTER 3

"There's a black market in space?"

A short laugh said space was similar to Earth in many ways, including piracy. "A very busy one. Across the entire galaxy. It's a huge problem, given that space is so vast. There's a concerted effort to reduce piracy but it's hard to catch thieves with so much space to hide in."

The alien relapsed into a moment of silence. "When I saw them following me I thought I could outrun them. My ship is fast." It shrugged again. "Guess they were faster."

Silence followed as we adjusted to what he'd said, Mac doing so before me. The soldier thing, again. Think on your feet if you want to stay alive. "Is your ship reparable?"

"Of course. The damage is minor, though it was enough to make me lose control. I tried to avoid settled areas of Earth, of course, and I believe I managed that well enough and the repairs will take no more than a few Earth days, after which I could normally be on my way."

"Normally?" Mac's eyebrows rose. "But not now?"

The alien gestured to himself and then to the hospital type bed he lay on and to the room itself. "It seems I was injured badly enough that it'll take a long time, perhaps weeks, to recover enough to pilot my craft once more, even though I'll be functional for some things. The ship is fully automated." His eyes narrowed. "But with the pirates knowing my route I can't depend on autopilot to the extent I have so far. I must be watchful. And I can't wait weeks to be on my way."

His look rested on Mac, ignoring me. Did he know Mac was the military person in the room? The in-charge guy? Of course he did. Mac exuded control and the kind of assurance only soldiers possess. "Billions will die if I can't get my cargo delivered in a timely manner."

"What are you saying?"

"I'm carrying medicine. Drugs. Drugs being the important word because legal, medicinal drugs can fetch as much on the black market as illegal ones. Often more because legal drugs are pure. And safe."

A sigh reached us. "There's an epidemic on Quintus Four." Mac's eyebrows rose in question. "A planet so far away it's on the fringes of galactic society. But there's a plague there now and everyone on Quintus Four will die if I can't get the antidote to them in time." He paused for effect. "My cargo is the antidote – the drugs the pirates are after. A week or so – a few weeks at most -- is all they have without the drugs in the cargo bay."

Mac nodded. A thoughtful look crossed his face. "I'm a pilot and I'm unemployed at the moment." The alien's huge black eyes glowed with hope. "But I know nothing about spaceships."

The alien pushed himself onto his elbows. It required effort but he managed. "All flying craft operate on the same basic principles so it's not that different from what you already know." The alien and Mac stared at one another. "I can teach you what else you need to know." The alien's eyes begged. How'd I thought he didn't show emotion? "Will you help?"

"You said billions will die." Mac rubbed the back of his neck. "That's unacceptable." He nodded shortly. "So, yes, I'll help if you think that together we can get the drugs delivered in time."

The alien beamed. It transformed him. "I'll speed things up. Make the mechanics work faster. It'll still be a couple Earth days before repairs can be completed but I'm sure they can be done in that time frame. Then we'll leave."

"What about food? I'm human, you know. I need human food. And a space suit. Do you have anything that'll fit me in case those pirates come after us again? And can you provide whatever else I might need?"

The alien waved a tiny, green hand to show how insignificant the questions were. "My ship was recently retrofitted. It can manufacture whatever you might require, no matter what species you are or what star system you are from."

"That's good to know." Mac looked around. "But what about accommodations? Is this a one-person ship?"

The alien looked insulted. "I'll have you know it can accommodate over a hundred beings of various species and has done so when I turned it into a yacht to transport beings to wherever they wished to go." Then he added, "Though I much prefer cargo that doesn't complain if the accommodations aren't luxurious enough."

"A couple of days, then. I'll be ready." Mac had one more question. "What can I call you? What's your name? If you have a name."

"I do." It then said something so long and

unpronounceable that we knew we'd never be able to say it.

Mac grinned. "I think the first sound you made was an 'Fr' though it's hard to know for sure. Anyway, I'll assume it was so I'll call you Frank. Is that okay?"

The alien indicated Frank would do as a name and we introduced ourselves and it appeared to have no difficulty with our names. Then Mac said he'd like to take a tour of the ship and I decided I did too for a very simple reason. This was the only chance I'd ever have to explore a flying saucer. A UFO. A spaceship.

We spent the next hour poking about the flying saucer until we pretty much knew its layout and how that maze of corridors worked. Then Mac said we should give Frank the time and solitude to rest and recuperate which he would do better if strange beings – us – were done wandering through his precious ship and possibly damaging it. Another pilot thing, I decided. It wouldn't have occurred to me to worry about damaging anything but he knew how attached pilots could get to their craft.

We returned to Cutters Gap. In the time we'd been in the spaceship the day had passed and it was growing dark though in town the night wasn't as deep as it had been in the valley. Mac turned to me. "I have pop and we can cook dinner together and eat while counting stars." He waited a moment and then added, "We can discuss stuff while we eat."

"Stuff?"

"Spaceships. Aliens. And other stuff."

Dinner was steaks on the tiny grill on his deck plus whatever else we found in his refrigerator. He cleaned it out, the small amounts of whatever was in there.

"Might as well eat it all. No knowing when I'll get back."

"Mine too. So it doesn't spoil while we're gone."

Mac checked the steaks. Deciding they were done, he flipped them onto plates already holding rolls and the remains of his refrigerator. Then he came to me and simply folded me in his arms, holding me warm and tight and rocking me back and forth as the breeze cooled the air. Comforting me. I wanted to stay there forever but knew he was holding me for a reason I probably wouldn't like.

The steaks were growing cold so we broke apart and started eating in silence. He found ice cream in the freezer compartment of his refrigerator when we were finished and served humongous portions of Chocolate Chunk swimming in chocolate sauce that we ate, still without speaking because we might as well finish what was in the freezer, too as I wondered what he was going to say that I would hate.

When the ice cream was gone we washed dishes side by side in his kitchen and then returned to the deck to sink into those chairs and put our feet on the railing and stare at the night as if it was the most interesting thing ever.

He finally spoke, going back to what I'd said. "You're not going. I won't allow it."

"Yes I am going. I want to go. I deserve to go. I've never traveled but I've always wanted to. Outer space will be awesome."

"This won't be a sightseeing trip. It's a mission and it's urgent. You've never traveled and you know nothing about flying or spaceships or about anything that might happen. You're not going."

I was angry. And growing angrier by the second. And sarcastic. "And you, with your military background, can do all those things with your hands tied behind your back."

"Pretty much." He refused to meet my look. Instead he checked out the first stars to come out, the ones bright enough to shine in the semi-dark of evening. "Even if I was willing to have you along – which I'm not -- it's Frank's ship and he's the Captain and he didn't say anything about both of us going. Just me. Because I'm a pilot and he needs one."

"We can ask him."

"We can." His voice said we wouldn't.

I wanted to scream. Instead I spoke reasonably, trying to hide my anger. "So you're saying there's no possibility of me going?"

"None."

He pulled me to him and I went willingly, damn him, anyway, for being such a perfect male that I couldn't resist and I didn't pull away. He was concerned for me and I was putty in his hands. I should have screamed at him and let him know how angry I was.

But what if things went sidewise once he was in space? What if he didn't return? Ever?

If that was the case then this would be the last time I'd get to feel him. His body. His warmth. That something special that made him who he was, something I couldn't describe but would know instantly no matter where we were or what was happening and the realization that I'd come to know him that well since he moved to the small town where I'd grown up shocked me. And kept me from complaining.

The next thing he did was pull me even closer if such was possible and we were kissing. Deeply. Thoroughly. When we drew apart, he said, "When I return, we'll talk."

"About what?"

"Stuff." Then he added, "Us."

The next thing I knew I was on my way to my own apartment, wondering what had just happened, what that kiss had meant and what we'd talk about upon his return, while telling myself the whole situation, whether intentional or not, wasn't fair. It didn't matter that I wasn't an experienced traveler. I should be going. I should be included. I deserved to be.

They were going somewhere across the galaxy. Far, far away and Mac had simply decided I couldn't go. He had no right to make decisions for me.

I'd never traveled. It had never bothered me before but now I thought about it I realized I wanted to. I wanted it very much and it looked like that wish wasn't going to be granted because I had no choice. None.

Or did I? Could I have a choice after all?

I stopped as if frozen as an idea came to me full blown and complete.

Frank had said his ship could accommodate a hundred beings of all kinds. Surely it could hold one smallish extra human while it flew among the stars. In such a ship there must be numerous hiding places where I could live during the trip and be comfortable until returning to Earth. It would be easy. All I had to do was get on board without being noticed and become a stowaway.

A stowaway. Like in a novel. I'd do it.

That's the beginning of *Spaceship Mercy*. I hope you like it and that you also like the entire book when it's published. It'll be on Amazon, published by Winged Publications, and will be free with Kindle Unlimited. So, until next time, I'm--

Florence Witkop